Matrimony Meltdown

by

Kathi Daley

This book is dedicated to my sister Christy for her time, encouragement, and unwavering support.

I also want to thank my super-husband Ken for allowing me time to write by taking care of everything else.

And of course I must thank the very talented Jessica Fischer for the cover art.

I so appreciate Bruce Curran, who is always ready and willing to answer my cyber questions.

Special thanks to Bobby Tobey, Joanne Kocourek, Janel Flynn, Sandra Kerr, Vivian Shane, and Melissa Nicholson for submitting recipes.

And, of course, thanks to the readers and bloggers in my life who make doing what I do possible, especially everyone who hangs out and likes and share my posts at Kathi Daley Books Group Page.

I also want to thank Carrie, Cristin, Brennen, and Danny for the Facebook shares, and Randy Ladenheim-Gil for the editing.

Books by Kathi Daley

Come for the murder, stay for the romance.
Buy them on Amazon today.

Zoe Donovan Cozy Mystery:
Halloween Hijinks
The Trouble With Turkeys
Christmas Crazy
Cupid's Curse
Big Bunny Bump-off
Beach Blanket Barbie
Maui Madness
Derby Divas
Haunted Hamlet
Turkeys, Tuxes, and Tabbies
Christmas Cozy
Alaskan Alliance
Matrimony Meltdown
Soul Surrender – *May 2015*
Heavenly Honeymoon – *June 2015*
Ghostly Graveyard – *October 2015*
Santa Sleuth – *December 2015*

Ashton Falls Cozy Cookbook

Paradise Lake Cozy Mystery:

Pumpkins in Paradise
Snowmen in Paradise
Bikinis in Paradise
Christmas in Paradise
Puppies in Paradise
Halloween in Paradise – *August 2015*

Whales and Tails Cozy Mystery:

Romeow and Juliet
The Mad Catter
Grimm's Furry Tail
Legend of Tabby Hollow – *September 2015*
Cat of Christmas Past – *November 2015*

Seacliff High Mystery:

The Secret
The Curse – *May 2015*
The Relic – *July 2015*
The Conspiracy – *October 2015*

Road to Christmas Romance:

Road to Christmas Past

Chapter 1

Sunday, July 12

I could just imagine the headline in tomorrow's newspaper: "Momzilla Strangled by Future Daughter-in-Law Two Weeks Before Wedding." Anyone who has ever spent what seemed like a lifetime planning a wedding would surely sympathize. Especially if their future mother-in-law was a demanding, controlling, and completely overbearing she-devil who insisted that every little detail mirror exactly the wedding that *she* had always dreamed of. For Zak's sake I have tried to get along with this woman, but it seems that the harder I try the harder she pushes.

"Zoe, are you even listening to me?" my future mother-in-law demanded with fire in her voice.

"Yes, Mrs. Zimmerman. I've heard every word you've said. It's just that I really have my heart set on Charlie and Scooter bringing the rings down the aisle. I even have matching bow ties for the boys."

For any of you who may not know, Scooter is a ten-year-old boy Zak has befriended and mentored and Charlie is my terrier mix and the very best friend I have in the world. I absolutely cannot imagine having my wedding without them.

"You cannot possibly be serious about having a dog in your wedding."

"Actually, I am very serious about having two dogs in the wedding. Charlie and Scooter are going to act as ring bearers and Bella and Alex are going to be the flower girls." I was referring to Zak's dog Bella and Scooter's friend Alex, a ten-year-old girl I'd met over Christmas and come to love. "It's going to be adorable."

"I'm sorry, but that simply won't do. Animals do not belong in a wedding party. Besides, I've already promised Zak's cousin Twyla that her son and daughter could be the ring bearer and flower girl."

I took a deep breath and counted to twenty. Ten simply wouldn't do.

"I'm sorry, but I've already asked Scooter and Alex. They're very excited about being in the wedding. I'm afraid I'm going to have to insist on this."

"Yes. Well, we shall see about that."

The woman turned and stormed away. I suppressed a groan as she threw her hands in the air before slamming the door to the back patio.

If I didn't love Zak so much I would kill him for leaving me alone with his mother. Of course I'm the one who assured him that I'd be fine in his absence. I was so certain of my ability to handle the woman who bore him that I practically demanded that he fly to the East Coast to take care of some last-minute business and then pick up the kids from the boarding school they both attended. Of course the trip was only supposed to last a few days. Four at the most. It certainly wasn't Zak's fault that his last-minute business trip had turned into a programing nightmare that had kept him away for almost a week.

Or was it?

Zak seemed even less thrilled than I was when his mother showed up at our front door two weeks ago. I couldn't help but notice the color drain from his face when she announced that she was going to stay until the wedding. It had occurred to me on more than one occasion that Zak's emergency trip to the opposite coast was just a tad too convenient. I hated to think he'd used a business emergency as an excuse to escape his demanding mother, but the more time I spent around the woman the more certain I was that escaping was a brilliant thing to do.

I headed upstairs to slip into a pair of running shorts and tennis shoes. I figured Charlie, Bella, and I would go for a run and then head over to the boathouse to hang out with Ellie and her dog Shep before the Wicked Witch of the Wedding found me again.

What I really needed, I decided, was some space. Space away from my future mother-in-law, space away from the demands of planning the wedding of the decade, space away from the circus my life had morphed into. I was so, so close to being out the door when the phone rang. Hoping it was Zak with good news about the software nightmare that had kept him away, I answered it without stopping to check the caller ID.

"Oh, good, you're home," my own mother, who I normally adore, greeted me.

"Actually, I was on my way out," I answered.

"I'm afraid we have a problem with the flowers," Mom continued. "I know you've been insisting on daisies, but I stopped by to look at a sample bouquet today and I just don't think daisies are going to go with your dress."

"Daisies are white. My dress is white. How could they not go together?" I asked.

"The dress I bought for you is elegant and formal. Daisies are such a common flower. I was thinking maybe orchids, or even lilies."

"But I like daisies," I insisted.

"Perhaps a mixed bouquet," Mom suggested. "I was thinking about something like white roses mixed in with white lilies and a daisy or two."

"Can we talk about this later?" I dodged. "I'm really late, so I have to run."

"Of course, dear. But we should talk about it soon. The flowers will need to be ordered."

"There's a huge bed of daisies on the side of the house, so I wouldn't worry about it. I love you." I hung up the phone before Mom could protest.

When exactly had I completely lost control of my own wedding? I wanted small, and what I ended up with was huge. I wanted to wear a simple cotton dress, and the dress I ended up with had such a full skirt and long train that I was pretty sure it weighed more than I did. I wanted daisies, but apparently a mixed bouquet would be more appropriate. And most of all I wanted Charlie, Bella, Scooter, and Alex as ring bearers and flower girls, but I had a sick feeling that Mother Zimmerman was having Twyla's demon spawn fitted for wedding clothes at that very moment.

I really wish you could've been here to witness the look on my face when I opened the front door to make my escape and witnessed a huge motor home pulling into my front drive. I could use words like *shocked*, *dismayed*, and *horrified*, but I'm certain these aren't strong enough to describe the level of terror I felt. I watched in stunned silence as the monstrosity pulled up to the front of the house and parked.

"Oh, good, the wedding planner is here," Mother Zimmerman informed me from just over my left shoulder.

"Wedding planner?" I screeched.

"Yes, dear. I'm sure you didn't think we were going to pull this wedding off without staff. I used my connections and managed to secure Pierre Bordeau, even though we have given him ridiculously short notice."

"Pierre Bordeau?" I asked.

"The wedding planner." Mother Zimmerman looked at me like I was dense. Apparently, *everyone* who was *anyone* had heard of Pierre Bordeau.

"But the wedding is planned," I argued.

"Don't be silly. The plans you and Zachary have made will never do. There are certain expectations that simply must be adhered to if we are to pull off such a high-profile wedding."

"Zak and I really wanted to keep it small and simple," I insisted.

"The folks from *Modern Day Celebrities* are expecting big and flashy, not small and simple."

"*Modern Day Celebrities*?" I knew *Modern Day Celebrities* was a popular magazine that prided itself on securing the exclusive rights to all of the big celebrity weddings. "*Modern Day Celebrities* is going to photograph our wedding?"

"You do realize who you are marrying?" Momzilla reminded me.

"I thought I did."

I felt my heart sink to my feet as Pierre exited the vehicle. He was a short, flashy man with a huge diamond on his left pinky finger and enough gold around his neck to pay for the beachfront mansion I lived in. Well, maybe that was an exaggeration, but the man was *extremely* accessorized.

"Pierre." Mother Zimmerman opened her arms to receive a kiss on each cheek from the perfectly groomed man. "I'd like you to meet the bride, Zoe Donovan."

Pierre looked me up and down. "This is the girl your Zachary is marrying?"

I held out my hand. "I'm happy to meet you." I'd plastered on a fake smile.

Pierre ignored my offer of a handshake. He returned his attention to the woman standing next to me. "Yes. I can see I got here just in time."

I gritted my teeth as Pierre introduced me to his two assistants, a tall and extremely thin woman named Julianna Something-or-other (I really wasn't listening) and a ridiculously dressed man named Longines. It seemed Julianna was to help with the scheduling and planning and Longines was the lucky man responsible for making sure I was photo ready on the big day.

"My, my," Longines tsk-tsked. "We really do have our work cut out for us, don't we?"

I wanted to ask who *we* were but kept my mouth shut for the time being.

"At the very least I'm thinking a cut and color. Maybe a chemical straightener. Is that curl natural?" Longines asked.

"Yes, my hair is natural, and yes, I like it, so no, I won't be coloring, cutting, or straightening it."

"I'm afraid big hair is out. Maybe something a bit longer in the front but short in the back. Perhaps collar length."

Over my dead body.

"I like my hair long," I insisted.

"No, I'm afraid that simply won't do. Short is trending," the man said in such a way as to indicate that his ridiculous statement settled things.

I wanted to send the man packing, but I could sense Mother Zimmerman tensing beside me.

"Are you all staying here?" I asked instead.

"Of course, dear," Mother Zimmerman informed me. "We are on such a short timeline as it is. I will admit it is going to be a bit crowded once Jimmy and the others get here."

"Jimmy?" I asked.

"Zak's best man."

I took a deep breath and tried to control my temper.

"Levi is Zak's best man," I informed the woman. "Zak asked him months ago."

"Levi is not a blood relative. A best man should be a blood relative. Levi can be one of the six groomsmen."

"Six groomsmen? We were actually planning to skip the groomsmen and go with just the maid of honor and best man."

"Don't be silly. That will never do." Mother Zimmerman seemed to notice my attire for the first time. "Are you going out?"

"I'm going to take the dogs for a run."

"Yes, about that. . . . I think it might be best if you took all the animals down to that shelter you run until after the wedding. Jimmy is allergic to cats and the dogs keep tracking dirt and sand in every time they go outdoors. When the decorators get here to prepare for the bridal shower we are going to want to keep the place as clean as we possibly can."

"I'm not going to have a bridal shower," I informed the woman.

"Don't be ridiculous. Of course you must. I plan to have it on Friday. It is part of the itinerary I left on your bedroom dresser."

"Itinerary?" I know I keep repeating everything Mother Zimmerman says to an annoying degree, but I was too upset to come up with an original thought.

"Please look it over by the end of the day. There really is a lot to get done in a very short period of time."

I opened my mouth to speak but found that I was too mad to respond. I simply bit my lip to hold back the tears I knew were lurking behind my eyelids and took off running. Bella and Charlie ran along beside me as we made our way down the beach and away from the locusts that had descended on the house Zak and I shared.

I ran along the beach, up the forest trail, and along the ridge that overlooked the lake. I ran until my lungs burned and my legs shook from exhaustion. I ran until the instinct to call off the wedding and run far, far away dulled to the point at which I could allow myself to remember how very much I wanted to marry Zak. I ran off the bulk of my anger and headed for Ellie and the boathouse.

"How mad do you think Zak will be if I strangle his mother?" I asked her after we'd settled in on the deck overlooking the lake.

"Pretty mad," Ellie said.

"I figured." I sat back in the patio chair I was lounging on.

I loved Zak and I loved living with him, but there were times I missed the simplicity of living in the tiny boathouse I'd called home before moving in with him. As I sat on the back deck that overlooked the crystal-clear lake, I found myself second-guessing every decision I'd made in the past year.

"Mother Zimmerman asked me if I knew who I was marrying," I volunteered. I looked at Ellie. "I thought I did, but now I'm not so sure."

"What are you talking about?" Ellie asked. "You know exactly who Zak is. You love him and he loves you. This whole wedding thing has turned into a bit of a nightmare," she added sympathetically, "but in a couple of weeks you'll be married, the nightmare will be over, and things will return to normal."

I tucked my bare feet up under my legs as I watched Bella, Charlie, and Shep chasing one another around on the beach. I loved this view, which I had always considered to be my little slice of heaven. The building was originally built by my grandfather to house his boat, but when the dam was opened to allow water to flow into the valley, the water level of the lake had dropped to the point where there was a significant amount of beach between the structure and the water. I'd asked if I could convert the space into a cabin of sorts and my grandfather had agreed. The boathouse was small, with just a living room, a small kitchen, a single bathroom, and a loft bedroom. But it had been mine, and I'd loved it. I'd missed my little home since moving into Zak's mansion just down the beach.

"I hope you're right," I responded. "But to be honest, I'm not sure I really stopped to think about who Zak is to the world outside of Ashton Falls. Mother Zimmerman has arranged for *Modern Day Celebrities* to photograph our wedding."

"Wow," Ellie commented. "That's really . . . wow."

"I wanted a nice, simple wedding with a few friends on the beach. I thought that was a reasonable expectation, but Mother Zimmerman almost has me convinced that it's our obligation to share the wedding of software phenomenon Zachary Zimmerman with the world."

"That's crazy. It's your wedding. You should be able to do what you want to do. Mrs. Zimmerman is taking advantage of the fact that Zak is out of town to push you around. Have you told him about the circus that's invaded his house?"

"No, not yet," I admitted. "I sort of hate to bother him. He's under a lot of pressure right now with the new software he's about to launch, and then to top that off, there's been a glitch in a program he installed a while back for one of his biggest customers. I hate to pile any more onto his plate."

"So don't. Why don't you and the animals come to stay at the boathouse until Zak gets back? He should be here in few days. Just ignore his mom and let him sort it out when he gets home."

"It'll be crowded. Are you sure it's okay?"

"It's more than okay. It'll be fun."

I leaned over and hugged Ellie. "Thanks. I think I'll do that. Not only are the wedding planner and his staff staying at the house but it looks like I can expect the arrival of a bunch of Zak's extended family."

Ellie stood up. "It's settled, then. Let's leave the dogs here and I'll come with you to get the cats and some of your things. We'll get everyone settled in and then we'll fire up the blender and make some margaritas. Levi is coming over later. I'll have him pick up something to BBQ."

"That sounds wonderful."

What sounded like a perfect idea turned out to be less than perfect after all. By the time Ellie and I got to the house, a swarm of cousins had descended on casa Zimmerman. They were everywhere, including in Zak's office. I sent Ellie to look for the cats while I dealt with the intruder.

"What are you doing in here?" I asked the tall man who was riffling through the files on Zak's desk.

The man had looked startled when I'd first walked in, but he quickly recovered. He smiled and held out his hand. "Jimmy Zimmerman. And you are . . . ?"

"Zoe Donovan." I ignored the outstretched hand. I wasn't sure this was a man I wanted to become too friendly with. For one thing, he looked like he'd just stepped off the cover of a magazine. There was no way this guy was real. He was probably some model Momzilla had hired to be Zak's best man.

"What are you doing in Zak's office?" I asked.

"Just looking for a pad of paper to make some notes," he innocently replied. "I figured I'd get started on the best man toast."

"I'm afraid there's been a misunderstanding. Zak has already asked his best friend, Levi, to be his best man. I hope you understand."

The man shrugged and headed toward the door. "Makes no never mind to me. I just do as I'm told."

I closed the door after he walked out and looked around the office. Zak was going to flip if he found out that someone had been going through his files. I was pretty sure he had his most important files locked up in the safe, but even the doodles of a software genius could be valuable. As much as I hated to admit it, I was beginning to rethink my inclination to abandon the house. I was afraid of what the locusts would do if there was no one around to keep an eye on things. I straightened the files on the desk, then locked the door behind me.

"Oh, good, you are back." Mother Zimmerman intercepted my attempt to quietly sneak down the hall to my bedroom. "I want you to meet Zak's cousin Eric and his wife, Cindy."

"I'm happy to meet you." I smiled at the friendly looking woman. I turned toward Eric and found myself recoiling from his obvious leer. Oh, great, just what I needed—a perv in the mix.

"Zak's best man, Jimmy, has arrived as well, but I'm not sure where he went off to," Mother Zimmerman added.

"Jimmy and I have met," I told the woman. "I found him in Zak's office. Zak is very particular about his office. I really think we need to keep people out of there."

"I'm sure Jimmy had a good reason to be in the office," Mrs. Zimmerman said defensively.

"He said he was looking for a writing pad to get started on his best-man speech. A speech he won't need because Levi is going to be Zak's best man," I reminded the woman.

"Yes. Well, we'll see."

"I'm keeping the office door locked, but it would help if you'd ask your guests to stay out of this wing of the house. All that's located down this hallway is Zak's office, our bedroom, and the guest rooms we plan to have Scooter and Alex stay in. There's no need for anyone to be down here."

Mrs. Zimmerman frowned. "Scooter and Alex are staying here?"

"Of course they're staying here. They're children. Where else would they stay?"

"I'm not sure we will have room for them. Zak's cousin Darlene will be arriving this evening, and I know Pierre said something about an intern who was going to be joining the party later in the day."

"We'll have room for Scooter and Alex," I said firmly. "You can have the wedding planner and his crew stay in town if we run out of bedrooms. Now I really must go find Ellie."

I headed across the hall and closed my bedroom door behind me.

"I found the cats," Ellie informed me. She was standing at the window, looking out onto the patio. "Who's that blond-haired man sitting in the lounger?"

I looked out the window. "That's Zak's cousin Jimmy."

"Wow."

"Yeah, he's a babe. A babe who was snooping around Zak's office. I have a really bad feeling about this whole thing. In spite of the fact that every self-preservation instinct I possess is telling me to run away, I feel like I have to maintain a presence. Who knows what would happen if I left completely? If you don't mind letting Bella, Marlow, and Spade stay with you, that would be a huge help."

"Of course. Are you sure?"

"I think that would be best. Charlie is used to a lot of chaos, but Bella and the cats, not so much."

"You know I'm happy to keep them. But are you sure you want to stay here in the midst of all this?" Ellie asked.

"I absolutely do not want to stay, but I feel like I should. My Zodar is telling me there's something not quite right about everything that's going on."

Ellie frowned. "What do you mean?"

"I don't know. It just seems odd that this Pierre Bordeau, who is supposed to be some big wedding planner to the stars, suddenly has time to fit in our wedding at the last minute. From what I can tell he's bringing in three staff members as well. That seems like overkill to me. And why are they here now? It's almost two weeks until the wedding. Why would they need to stay here all that time?"

"Maybe Mrs. Zimmerman is paying them a *lot* of money."

"Maybe. It just doesn't make sense that four people would need to spend two weeks onsite preparing for an event that's going to take place on the back patio."

"Yeah, I guess that is a bit odd," Ellie agreed.

"And then there's the Zimmerman family. I get the fact that Zak's family doesn't live in the area and needs to travel here, but unless they're coming from overseas, most family members show up for a wedding the day before, maybe two days if they're traveling a great distance. Cousin Jimmy, Cousin Eric, and Eric's wife Cindy are all already here, and Mrs. Zimmerman indicated that another cousin named Darlene would be arriving by the end of the day. Why in the world did Mrs. Zimmerman have them come to Ashton Falls now?"

"I take it all the extra people have you rattled?"

"Of course they have me rattled. It's taking every ounce of control I have to fight the instinct to head for the border."

"Maybe that's it," Ellie pointed out. "You've speculated all along that Mrs. Zimmerman doesn't support Zak's desire to marry you. Maybe she's trying to run you off."

I hated to admit it, but that actually made sense. Zak didn't know I knew that his mom had almost had a coronary when she found out about the engagement. Zak had tried to pretend that she was thrilled, but I'd overheard a conversation he'd had with her just after he'd informed her of our plans, and it had sounded to me like she was anything but delighted. In fact, she'd been quite hysterical about the fact that "marrying a mess like Zoe Donovan" was going to be a decision Zak would live to regret.

In all fairness, I *was* a bit of a mess when Zak first started dating me, but I've grown up in the past year and a half. Mostly. I suppose I still had a Zoe moment every now and then, but according to Zak, emotional instability in the face of enthusiastic jealousy really is one of my most enduring traits.

"You know she's pushing for a prenup," I told Ellie.

"And you don't want one?"

"Actually, I suggested one, but Zak is adamant that we won't have one. He said everything he'd worked for since the moment he met me in the seventh grade had been for us."

"Aw. That's so sweet."

"It is sweet. I love Zak and I'm not going to let his mother scare me off. Let's pack up the cats and move them to your place. Charlie and I will stay and have dinner with you and Levi, but we really should come back to keep an eye on things."

"Whatever you think is best."

Chapter 2

Later that evening I sat with Levi and Ellie on the boathouse deck. He'd brought his dog Karloff with him, and the four dogs were having the time of their lives playing on the beach. Marlow and Spade seemed glad to be in a quiet yet familiar territory, quickly making themselves comfortable on Ellie's bed.

Maybe it was the margaritas, maybe it was the peaceful surroundings, or perhaps it was the company of good friends, but I felt myself relax for the first time in weeks. Levi had built a fire in the pit, which provided both warmth and atmosphere to the summer evening.

"I forget how much I miss this," I said as I watched the sun set into the lake.

"You have virtually this same view," Ellie pointed out.

"I know, but it seems like things have been so hectic this summer that I haven't taken the time to just sit and watch the world go by. Remember when the three of us used to get together every Wednesday for a hump day celebration?"

"Yeah," Ellie agreed. "I have to say I miss that too. But we've all been really busy lately. Business at Ellie's Beach Hut has doubled since last year. Which is good," she clarified. "But Kelly and I are having a hard time taking time for ourselves. We hired some seasonal help, but I think what we really need is a shift manager. It's hard for the two of us to cover the longer summer hours."

I looked at Levi. "Seems to me you're off this summer. Maybe you can help Ellie out at the Hut."

"I offered to, but she didn't want me underfoot," Levi informed me.

"I guess I can't blame her for that," I teased. "I usually shoo Zak away if he decides to spend too much time at the Zoo." I referred to the wild and domestic animal rescue and rehabilitation clinic I run.

"Have you talked to Zak today?" Levi asked.

"He called earlier. He sounded really tired, so I didn't mention the circus that's invaded his house."

"He still having a problem with the software?"

"He didn't go into detail, but I could tell by the tone in his voice that things weren't going well. The timing of the problem with the software couldn't have come at a worse time. Not only is he worried about the wedding but on top of everything else he's concerned that a problem with existing software could affect the introduction of his new program."

"Zak will figure it out," Levi assured me. "He always does. In the meantime, how can Ellie and I help you deal with the wedding fiasco?"

"This is a good start," I said. "I think I'm going to spend the day at the Zoo tomorrow. Jeremy and Tiffany have been great about picking up the slack lately, but I miss being down there and hanging out with the animals."

"I heard you're up to ten bear cubs," Ellie noted as she stared at her bare feet in the sand.

"Yeah, we've had a bumper crop this year. It's sad that there are so many displaced babies. It makes me worry about the ones we don't find and save."

"Do you know what happened to the moms?" Ellie asked.

"A variety of things. A couple of the cubs were orphaned when their mom was hit by a car. One of the cubs was brought to us by a hunter who legally killed the mom. I wasn't sure what to think about that. On one hand, I was outraged that the man would hunt bear for sport. On the other, he could have left the cub to fend for itself. He claimed he didn't see the cub until after he killed the mom."

"That's so sad," Ellie said.

"Yeah. I love what I do, but most of the animals we work with come to us as the result of one sort of tragedy or another."

I yawned and stretched. It had been a long day and I had a feeling the next was going to be equally long and stressful. "I guess I should get going," I announced.

I bent over to slip on my shoes. "Maybe we can do dinner again tomorrow. My plan is to stay away from the house as much as possible while still popping in and out at random times to keep an eye on things. Hopefully as long as I maintain a presence, people will stay out of our bedroom and Zak's office."

"It does seem a little suspect that this cousin of Zak's was riffling through his paperwork," Levi commented as he got up and began to gather the empty dishes.

"There's something that just isn't quite right about the guy."

"Like what?" Levi asked.

"For one thing, he's too pretty to be real. If I didn't know better I'd say that Momzilla hired him to be in the wedding so the pictures would turn out just so." I looked at Levi. "No offense. You know you're a total babe, but this guy . . . well, this guy looks like an airbrushed supermodel."

"Zak is never going to let some random guy take Levi's place in the wedding," Ellie promised me.

"Yeah. I know you're right. Still, until he gets back I think I'll keep an eye on the guy. My Zodar is telling me that there's something off about him."

"If I had to guess I'd say you're just tired and stressed out, which is making you see evil intent where there is none," Ellie offered. "I doubt even Zak's mother would hire someone to pretend to be Zak's cousin. The guy most likely did need something to write on and figured the office was as good a place as any to look."

"Maybe." I looked toward the water, where the dogs were standing in a line looking out over the lake. It really was the perfect summer evening. Clear and warm, without even a hint of a breeze to mar the glassy reflection of the surrounding mountains on the surface of the water.

"By the way," Ellie said as I called Charlie over, "I ran into Tiffany yesterday and she asked me about a bachelorette party. I know you said you didn't really want to do anything, but how about having just a few friends come here to the boathouse?"

I thought about it. I supposed it could be fun to spend an evening with Ellie, Tiffany, and maybe a couple of others.

"Nothing fancy?" I asked.

"Just a simple dinner and drinks on the deck. Like what we're doing now, only with a few additional women," Ellie said. "I'll let you manage the guest list."

"Well, okay. I guess I could go for a BYOD gathering of sorts as long as we keep it small."

"BYOD?" she asked.

"Bring your own dog."

Ellie laughed. "Sounds perfect."

"As long as we're talking prewedding affairs, I was informed today that I'm having a bridal shower on Friday. I already communicated to Mother Zimmerman that I absolutely did not want to have a shower, but apparently my wanting or not wanting one is completely irrelevant. I'm still hoping to put an end to the whole thing, but in the event that I'm unable to stop this train wreck, I absolutely want you to be there. I have a feeling the woman hasn't even thought about inviting my actual friends."

"No, I haven't received an invitation, and yes, I will absolutely plan to be there if you can't figure out a way around it."

"Thanks. I may need someone to restrain me if she decides to play pin-the-tail-on-the-bride or some other lame game."

"I doubt your future mother-in-law will have that kind of a shower. So far she's been all about putting on a high-profile but classy affair she can invite her upper-class friends to," Ellie assured me.

"Yeah, you're probably right. It's just that this whole wedding planner thing really has me in a tailspin. The man looked at me like I was dirt, and don't get me started on his assistant, Longines. He wants me to cut and color my hair."

"Really? What color?" Ellie asked.

"I didn't let him get that far."

"Maybe you should at least see what he has in mind," Ellie suggested.

I glared at her.

"I didn't say you had to take his advice, but if he does this for a living he might be able to give you some valuable tips."

"The guy looks a lot like fat Elvis. I really can't imagine how he can make a living advising others when he's such a mess himself."

"Fat Elvis?" Levi laughed. "Really?"

"Just wait until you meet him."

Levi followed me into the boathouse. He set the dishes he was carrying on the counter and turned to give me a good-bye hug just as his cell phone rang. He took his phone out of his pocket and looked at the caller ID.

He frowned.

"Who is it?" Ellie asked as she closed the screen door behind us.

"I'm not sure. I don't recognize the number." Levi pushed the answer button on his phone. "Levi Denton."

I watched his face as he listened. His expression morphed from confusion to surprise to delight to terror. So far all he'd done was listen to the person on the other end, but I had a strong feeling this after-hours phone call had the potential to be life-changing.

"I'm honored," Levi finally said. "And yes, I'm interested. What does the timeline look like?" He frowned. "That soon?" He bit his lower lip, a nervous habit he'd had since he was a kid.

"Yeah. I understand." He looked at me and raised one eyebrow. "I'll get back to you in a few days." Levi hung up and put his phone back in his pocket.

"Who was that?" Ellie asked.

"Brick Kincade."

I knew Kincade was the head football coach at the state college. Levi had met him at a coaches' camp a few years earlier and they'd stayed in contact.

"What did he want?" Ellie asked.

"He offered me a job."

"A job?" Ellie screeched after a stunned pause.

"As the assistant to the offensive coordinator," Levi confirmed.

"As the assistant to the offensive coordinator at the college he coaches at?" Ellie rambled.

Levi looked at Ellie. He took her hand. "I know this is sudden. It's a lot to take in, and there's a lot to consider."

I could see Ellie was about to cry, so I filled the void. "*Are* you considering it?"

Levi looked at me. "I think I have to. It's a huge opportunity. One I may never get again."

"But it's almost four hundred miles away," Ellie finally said.

"I know. Believe me, I know. I don't want to move, but . . ."

I knew how much Levi loved coaching, but I also knew how much he loved Ashton Falls and Ellie. Not that Ellie couldn't move with him, but she did own her own business. . . .

"When do you have to make up your mind?" Ellie asked.

"They want to know by the end of the month."

"That's not a lot of time," Ellie pointed out.

"No," Levi agreed. "It isn't."

The three of us stood in silence for a few minutes. I'd never thought about what I'd do if Zak decided to move for work. Go with him, I supposed, but I knew Ashton Falls held a big chunk of my heart, as did

Levi and Ellie. Things would never be the same without them.

"I really should get going." I could see Levi and Ellie needed time alone to talk. I hugged Ellie as tightly as I could and then turned and hugged Levi.

"I'll call you tomorrow," I said to Levi.

He nodded.

I wished I could be there for my friends the way they had been there for me earlier in the evening, but I really had no idea what to say. They had a hard decision to make. A decision I knew wasn't going to come easily.

Charlie and I walked back along the beach. The distance between the boathouse and Zak's mansion was over a mile by road but less than a quarter of a mile by beach. I'd made the trip between the two properties in just a few minutes many times in the past, but tonight I took my time. I couldn't help but dread returning to the house of insanity I'd fled earlier in the day.

I stood on the beach, looking back toward the house once we'd arrived on the property. If I timed it correctly and no one was in the kitchen, I could sneak in the back door and make my way up the back staircase, avoiding the locusts that had descended on casa Zimmerman altogether. As I studied the house and considered my timing, I noticed that the light in Zak's office was on. I frowned. I knew I'd locked the door before I'd left the house earlier in the day.

"We'd better check it out," I said to Charlie. He looked at me and wagged his tail. I'm sure he had no idea what I was planning, but he seemed game for whatever I wanted to do.

Luckily, we managed to sneak in the back door and up the stairs without being seen. We made our way to Zak's office and tried the door. It was locked. I went to my bedroom and got the key Zak kept in a secret compartment in his nightstand. By the time we returned and unlocked the door the light had been turned off and the office was empty.

I entered the room and closed the door behind Charlie and me. Nothing appeared to have been disturbed on the surface, but the light in the room had definitely been on, so someone had to have broken in for some reason. I sat down in Zak's desk chair and considered my options.

I could call Zak and tell him that someone had been snooping around in his office. There wasn't anything he could do about it from the opposite side of the country, and I really didn't want to distract him from the job he was doing. I hoped he'd get things wrapped up in a day or two at the most and return to Ashton Falls before I strangled his mother.

I could sleep in the office, but that seemed needlessly uncomfortable. Chances were that whoever had broken in knew I was home and wouldn't try again until I was out. Then again, they might just be waiting until I fell asleep.

I looked at the clock. It was late, but not that late. Zak would most likely still be awake. I picked up the phone and dialed his number.

"Zoe, I'm so glad you called," Zak answered. "I called the house earlier and Mom said you were out, so I tried your cell, but it was turned off."

I frowned and pulled my cell out of my pocket. "Dead battery," I explained. "I was at the boathouse having dinner with Ellie and Levi." I decided not to bring up Levi's job offer just yet. Zak had enough on his mind. "How are things going with you?"

"Slowly." Zak sighed. "I thought I had the problem fixed, but it seems like as soon as I get one thing fixed, another problem pops up. I'm beginning to suspect someone has gained access to the software through a back door. So far I haven't been able to discover exactly how that was accomplished, but it's evident someone is messing with the programming as fast as I can repair it. It almost feels like I've stumbled into some huge game I'm afraid I'm losing."

"Who would do something like that?"

"Honestly, I have no idea. Whoever is accessing the system is very skilled. There are a few hackers I know of who are capable of doing what's being done, but I don't understand why any of them would bother with this particular system. It's not linked to anything like military secrets or financial information."

"Maybe someone really is playing a game with you," I suggested.

"But why?"

"Maybe it's a competitor. You're all set to launch your new software in the fall; maybe someone wants to cast doubt on your programming capabilities, or maybe they're trying to distract you so you don't have time to complete your testing."

Zak was silent for a moment. "Yeah, maybe. How are things going between you and my mom?"

I could sense the worry in his voice. The poor guy sounded like he was at the end of his rope. The last thing I wanted to do was add to his stress, so I took a deep breath and told him a lie.

"Things are going fine," I answered. "I think we're really starting to get along. You were right. We just needed some time to settle into a comfort zone."

"That's good." Zak let out the breath he must have been holding. "I was worried the two of you had been at each other's throats since I left. Mom can be somewhat . . ."

"Overzealous," I finished for him.

"Exactly."

"Well, you can relax," I reassured him. "We're getting along just fine."

"I'm glad to hear that because it looks like I most likely won't be home until the weekend."

I felt my heart sink. "I miss you."

"Not as much as I miss you," Zak said.

"Have you filled the kids in on your change of plans?" I asked.

"I spoke to both of them. They're naturally disappointed about the delay, but they seemed to understand. They really are great kids."

"They really are," I agreed. "I can't wait for our trip to Heavenly Island."

Zak and I had discussed a honeymoon and decided that because Scooter and Alex would only be with us a short time, we wanted to spend as much time with them as we could. Zak had a friend who owned an all-inclusive resort geared toward families just off the Florida coast. He'd offered us a four-bedroom house for our stay, so we planned to take the kids and have a real family vacation.

"Yeah, about that . . ." Zak hedged.

I knew where he was going next but couldn't let myself believe it.

"Mom is giving us a trip for our wedding present. I spoke to her earlier and she's very excited about it."

"A trip?" I asked.

"I'm afraid so."

"A trip we can take later?" I offered hopefully. "After the kids go back to school?"

"Afraid not. She won't tell me where we're going, but she did say the trip was booked and paid for. We leave the day after the wedding."

"Surely you told her that we had other plans," I tried desperately.

"I did."

"And?"

"She launched into her ungrateful-son routine. I tried to stay firm, but then she reminded me of all the sacrifices she made for me after my dad left. I could tell she was crushed that I wasn't as thrilled about her gift as she was."

I sat quietly. I picked up a pen from the surface of Zak's desk and began to rapidly click it opened and closed. I figured if I waited long enough he'd tell me that he'd stood firm and we were taking the trip we had planned with the kids.

"Maybe we can get Levi and Ellie to take the kids to Heavenly Island. You mentioned you were thinking of asking them to come along anyway."

What happened to my mature, self-confident fiancé? The Zak I knew was selfless and would sacrifice his own desires to meet *my* needs at the drop of a hat, and I couldn't believe he was putting his mother's wishes before mine. Who was this man?

"I have to go. I'll talk to you tomorrow."

I hung up. The phone rang a few seconds later. I knew it was Zak, but it seemed that selfish, jealous, immature Zoe was back. I ignored it and headed to bed to cry myself to sleep.

Chapter 3

Monday, July 13

"Mothers and sons often have complicated relationships," my assistant, Jeremy Fisher, explained to me when I arrived at Zoe's Zoo the next morning.

"I'll say. Zak seemed like a completely different person on the phone last night. I couldn't believe he let his mom manipulate him the way he did."

"He lets you manipulate him all the time," Jeremy pointed out as Charlie and I helped him clean the bear cage.

"That's different. He loves me."

"I'm sure he loves his mother as well."

Jeremy replaced the water tubs with freshly cleaned metal containers as I finished up the ground work. We'd done this so many times that we had a well-choreographed routine that required little communication as we worked.

"The woman is a controlling, demanding witch. I can't believe Zak is caving into her the way he seems to be. He has to see how she's manipulating the situation."

Jeremy stopped what he was doing and looked at me. "You told me that Zak's dad left when he was young and his mother had to work two jobs to support him. I'm sure he feels indebted to her, and I'd also be willing to bet he feels protective toward her. She was there for him when he needed her, and it makes sense that he wants to find a way to repay her. Yes, she seems to be pushing him around, but she's also pushing you around, and you're the most stubborn, assertive woman I know."

Jeremy had a point. Maybe I *was* being too hard on Zak. He was dealing with a lot of stress, and having a fiancée on meltdown couldn't be helping the situation. I knew I needed to call him back to calmly discuss a solution to the situation. It was obvious that some sort of compromise was in order.

"I've been thinking about the lab puppies that came in last week," Jeremy said, changing the subject after we'd worked quietly for several minutes. "I had a man come in yesterday who was interested in adopting both of them. I know we discussed not adopting them out together because they're so hyper and we anticipated it would take someone with a firm hand to handle them both. I've done some checking, and not only does the guy have a large piece of land so the dogs could run around to get the exercise they need but he has a lot of experience training dogs as well."

"Did you discuss the behavior issues we're having with them?"

"We did. The guy wants to train the dogs to hunt. Duck hunting, to be specific. I know it's not something you like to hear because you don't support hunting of any kind. But a life as field dogs could be a good one for energetic dogs like the lab brothers. It's what they were bred for. I think we should consider it."

I hesitated.

"Not allowing this man to adopt the pups won't keep him from hunting; it'll just keep the pups from having a home that appears to be a perfect fit for them," Jeremy reminded me.

"Yeah. You're right. If you think it's a good placement, go ahead. I trust your judgment."

"I'm glad you said that because he's coming back this afternoon. I think it would be best if I handle everything."

"Are you afraid I'm going to get up on my soapbox and subject the man to my nonviolence-toward-all-things-large-and-small speech?"

"I'm absolutely afraid you'll do that at a minimum."

"Don't worry; you can handle the adoption. Speaking of adoptions, did you nail down a date for the clinic next month?"

"I thought we'd go for the third Saturday. You'll be back from your honeymoon by then, and I'm sure Tiff and I will need the extra help. I confirmed that we'll be able to get a permit to do it in the park. I'm going to set up some big tents for additional shade in case it's hot that day."

"That's a good idea. Let's see if we can set up near the gazebo. Maybe we can use the structure as well. If you want to go ahead and make up an ad to send to nearby newspapers I'll take a look at it and send it off."

"Actually, there's a rough draft on your desk."

I found that I was really looking forward to the event. I always welcomed the opportunity to meet and establish relationships with animal lovers from out of the area.

"By the way, Jessica told me that Ellie called to invite her to a bachelorette party. I thought you didn't want to have one."

"I didn't, but Ellie promised me a small gathering at the boathouse. We discussed keeping it to no more than eight women. I hope that's doable. I know Ellie has invited Jessica, Tiffany, and Kelly. If you add Ellie and me, that's five already."

"I'm sure Ellie will keep it small. She knows you don't want a big event. It was nice of you to include Jessica. She doesn't have a lot of friends in Ashton Falls, and I know it meant a lot to her to receive the invitation. She doesn't have a dog to bring, however, so I hope that part was optional."

I laughed. "There'll be plenty of dogs even if she doesn't bring one. Tiffany doesn't have a dog either."

After I finished at the Zoo, I decide to go by Donovan's, the general store my dad owns, to say hi. While my mom had gone just a bit wedding crazy, Dad was still wonderfully detached from the whole thing. It would be nice to visit with him when Mom wasn't around to bring up wedding plans. I felt bad that I had been avoiding the pair the past few months, but a person who has been driven to the edge of wedding insanity can only be polite for so long with those who want to add to the craziness before being driven totally over the edge.

"Zoe, what brings you here?" Dad asked after kissing me on the cheek and bending over to pet Charlie.

"I'm hiding." I took a few minutes to fill him in on the fiasco going on over at casa Zimmerman.

"Whatever you do, don't tell your mother," Dad warned. "If she realizes the woman has hired a wedding planner she'll be over there before you know it to defend her territory."

"What about *my* territory?" I complained.

"Yes, well, it does seem that the female of the species goes a little crazy when the word *wedding* is mentioned."

"Not all women," I defended myself.

"Oh, really? Do you remember the end result of the small wedding your mom and I planned to have until a certain daughter of ours got involved?"

Dad was right. He and Mom had wanted small until I turned their wedding into a major affair. Still, while the wedding I created might have been larger than Dad and Mom had set out to have, it was nothing like the circus the moms were orchestrating right before my horrified eyes.

"I wonder if getting Mom involved might not be a good idea," I considered. "Maybe the two moms will distract each other to the point that they'll leave me alone."

"I doubt it will work out that way," Dad said sympathetically.

"Yeah, probably not. Still, maybe I should tell her, so it doesn't look like I'm intentionally keeping things from her."

Dad shrugged. "It's your call."

I picked a piece of penny candy out of the jar and popped it into my mouth. Charlie looked up at me as he waited patiently for his treat. I reached behind the counter for the bag of dog treats Dad always kept on hand.

"Something else on your mind?" he asked.

"Lots of things," I answered. "The least of which are all the strange things going on at the house since the Zimmerman cousins and the wedding planner and his crew arrived."

"Strange how?"

"For one thing, I found Zak's cousin Jimmy riffling through the paperwork on Zak's desk. He said he was looking for a writing pad, but he looked guilty when I walked in. I locked the door when I left and I've kept it locked, but when I got home last night I noticed that there was a light on in the office. By the time I got upstairs and retrieved the key whoever was in the office was gone. I didn't notice anything out of place, so I relocked the door and went to bed."

I decided to leave out the part about my disaster of a conversation with Zak. I'd called him after my talk with Jeremy, but he hadn't answered. I'd left a message, but he hadn't called back yet. I had to admit that had me more than just a little worried.

"I went into the office this morning to check on things before I went out," I continued. "I noticed that the files that had been on the desk were in a different order than the way I'd left them."

Dad furrowed his brow.

"And it looks like the office hasn't been the only room violated. When I went up to our room to go to bed last night I noticed the alarm clock was unplugged. I know it was plugged in when I left the room earlier in the day. It looked like someone had pulled out the bedside table and the plug had pulled away from the wall. The table had been moved back into place, but you could see the mark on the carpet where the previous location had left an indentation."

"Maybe you should come to stay with Mom, Harper, and me until this whole thing is over," Dad suggested.

"No. I need to maintain a presence in the house so that whoever is snooping around will think twice about being where they shouldn't be. I figure if I pop in and out at random times it might keep whoever has been snooping from doing it again. I took Bella and the cats to Ellie's, but I'm keeping Charlie with me. He'd warn me if someone tried to sneak up on me. I'll lock my bedroom door when I go up for the night, unless I decide to sleep in the office."

"Why would you sleep in there?"

"If someone is looking for anything, chances are it's something Zak is working on. His new software program is worth hundreds of millions of dollars."

"Surely Zak didn't leave any notes pertaining to that lying around," Dad said.

"I'm sure he didn't, but that doesn't mean that Zak's smaller ideas, or even some discarded ones, aren't worth something to someone. I just wish I could keep an eye on the bedroom and the office at the same time."

"You need a baby monitor," Dad suggested. "When Harper was born your mom and I both wanted to keep her close, but we also wanted to have our own space. The monitor works great. We can hear everything that's going on in her room, but we don't need to worry about our movements disturbing her."

"That's brilliant. I'll put a baby monitor in the office so I can hear if someone breaks in during the night."

"I started carrying them in the store after Harper was born." Dad walked over to a shelf, took down a box, and handed it to me. "This is a top-of-the-line model. You should be able to hear a fly land on the desk if you have it turned all the way up."

I hugged him. "Thanks, Dad."

"About your mom . . ."

"I'll call her. She's going to hear about the wedding planner. I want her to hear it from me."

We paused our conversation when a customer walked in. Dad rang up the man's purchase, then turned his attention back to me.

"So how is Zak doing with his computer glitch?" Dad asked.

I explained that someone was creating new problems at about the same rate Zak was fixing the existing ones. "He said it feels like someone is playing a game with him."

"Sounds like it," Dad agreed. "Does he know what he's going to do?"

"Not that he's said."

"He's a smart guy. He'll figure it out," Dad assured me. "Still, it must be frustrating to feel like someone has you jumping through hoops."

"Yeah, he's frustrated and confused. He has no idea why someone with the hacking skills the person involved obviously has would even bother to hack into this software."

"Sort of sounds personal," Dad commented. "Like maybe the hacking has more to do with Zak than the software."

"Yeah, that's what I thought. Maybe someone is trying to stop the wedding by keeping Zak tied up."

"Why would anyone want to stop the wedding?" Dad asked.

"I don't know."

"I doubt anyone is trying to stop the wedding, but someone may be trying to stop Zak from launching his new software program," Dad said.

"It occurred to me that it could be a competitor. Maybe someone who's close to launching a similar product but needs more time. I don't know what Zak is going to do if he can't shut this guy down."

"Do you think the break-ins to Zak's office are in any way related to the hacker problem?" Dad asked.

I thought about it. "I'm not sure how, but it would make sense. Maybe someone just wanted to get Zak out of the house so they could steal the plans for his new design."

"Are the plans in his office?"

"I'm not sure. We never really discussed it. I do know that he has a hidden safe that's not only locked but alarmed. He keeps all his most important papers and computer programs in there. And he also has a couple of different lockboxes scattered around the country. He could have stashed his blueprints for the program anywhere."

After I left the store I called my mom and told her about the wedding planner and then headed over to the Beach Hut. As predicted, when Mom heard that Zak's mom had hired a wedding planner without even consulting her, she went ballistic. I was pretty sure I was going to return home to bloodshed, so I decided to get a dose of Ellie's special blend of comfort and soothing before I took on the moms.

"What's wrong?" she asked the moment I walked through the door.

"Nothing really. Charlie and I just need to spend some time with a friendly face before we head into the lion's den."

"Things are worse?" Ellie asked.

"I think they're about to get that way. I decided to tell my mom about the wedding planner."

Ellie asked her assistant, Kelly, to cover for her. Then she grabbed a soda for each of us and led me out to one of the tables that were set up on the pier for the summer. It was a beautiful day, and the beach was filled with couples and families enjoying a day in the sun. I had to hand it to Ellie; she had picked the perfect location for the lakeside sandwich and BBQ shop.

"How did your mom take the news?" Ellie asked as soon as we were seated.

"Not well. She was so mad that she kept switching between English and French, but I think I got the gist of it. My mom can be such a sweetie, but she can be a barracuda as well. I almost feel sorry for Zak's mom."

"Seriously?"

"I said *almost*."

"Do you think your mom has a tactical advantage over Zak's mom?"

"I do. She's going to eat both Mrs. Zimmerman and her wedding planner alive. I bet she already has Pierre Bordeau in tears."

Ellie laughed. "Maybe I should take off early and come with you to the house. It sounds like it's going to be quite a show."

I smiled. Leave it to Ellie to find the fun in such a stressful situation.

"By the way," Ellie added as a pair of boys on skateboards zipped past us, "a woman came in earlier asking about the wedding. She wanted to know all about it and she asked where you and Zak live."

I frowned. "Woman? What woman?"

"She said her name was Bridget. She had a look about her that suggested press. I'm afraid your quiet little wedding is going to turn into a paparazzi palooza, especially now that the wedding planner to the stars is involved."

"Fantastic," I said sarcastically. "That's just what I need. More press."

"I guess it comes with the territory. You *are* marrying someone famous."

"I'm not marrying anyone famous. I'm marrying Zak."

"He was voted the fourth most eligible bachelor in the country," Ellie reminded me.

"I don't want to talk about it."

"You may not want to talk about it, but that doesn't make it any less true."

"How did things go with you and Levi after I left last night?" I decided a change in subject was definitely in order.

Ellie sighed. "I'm not sure. We talked. It was civil. I know as his girlfriend I should be supportive and enthusiastic about this opportunity, but I'm not. I love Levi. I can't imagine not having him in my life every single day. But I have a home and a business I love." Ellie looked directly at me. "And I have a best friend I can't be without. Maybe it's selfish, but I want it all."

"It's not selfish," I assured her. "I can't imagine you and Levi not being here. In my wildest dreams I never suspected that the three of us—the four of us, now that we have Zak—wouldn't grow old together."

"Me too."

"Does it seem like he's *actually* considering this now that he's had time to let it sink in?"

"It does." Ellie sighed again. "He explained to me that it's every high school coach's dream to move on to the college arena."

"And he knows you don't want to move?"

She nodded. "He pointed out that four hundred miles isn't really that far, but we both know that it's *too* far. We can try the long-distance thing, but I doubt it will work in the long run."

"I suppose he could come home on the weekends."

"That might work for part of the year, but during the season there are games on the weekends," Ellie said.

"Yeah, I guess that's true."

"If you ask me," Ellie looked directly at me, "I don't think Levi really wants to move either. I think he's flattered to be asked, and I'm sure thoughts of a college coaching gig leading to bigger things is in the forefront of his mind, but I'm hoping that once he has time to consider everything he would be giving up, he'll decide that Ashton Falls High School is the perfect job for the long haul." Ellie attempted to speak with conviction, but her words came out hollow.

I laced my fingers through Ellie's in an offer of support. We sat quietly and looked out over the lake. Suddenly my wedding drama seemed insignificant. I don't know what I'd do if I lost Levi or, even worse, Levi and Ellie. I know that having them move away wouldn't be the same as losing them, but the three of us had been a best friend trio since kindergarten. Losing one or both of them would be like losing a piece of my soul.

Chapter 4

The wedding planning staff had made themselves scarce by the time I got home. Zak's cousins had decided to head to the beach, and the house was relatively quiet, with the exception of the slightly raised voices of Zak's mom and mine. They had taken their discussion out onto the patio, so I took advantage of the empty house to sneak into the office to hide the baby monitor. Now all I had to do was keep the other end with me at all times, and if someone tried to break in I'd be able to catch them red-handed. Provided I was home when the break-in occurred of course.

I planted the listening device in Zak's office, then decided to brave the moms and join them out on the patio.

"Zoe, I'm glad you're here," Mom greeted me. "Have a seat so we can chat."

Neither Zak's mom nor my own seemed to show any signs of blood or bruising, so maybe things were going better than I'd anticipated. I sat down next to my mom and waited.

"Helen and I have been talking about the wedding," Mom began. "I think we've come to an agreement as to how we're going to proceed from this point."

"So no wedding planner?" I asked hopefully. I wasn't sure yet if this was going to be better for me or not.

"I didn't say that," Mom corrected. "Helen has made a good point in that there really are a lot of details that still need to be ironed out, and having a professional staff to help with the specifics would make our job a lot easier."

"What details?" I asked. "All I want is a simple wedding on the beach with a few family and friends. This doesn't have to be complicated."

Mom and Helen glanced at each other. Uh-oh; I could see they were planning to team up on me. The glance they shared screamed conspiracy. Maybe Zak and I should elope. Vegas was hot during the summer, but perhaps Tahoe? I could picture it now: Zak and me standing on a white sand beach with only Levi and Ellie, Scooter, Alex, Bella, and Charlie. It would be perfect.

"Helen and I are just entering into the specifics of what we'd like to see," Mom interrupted my daydream. "You have to keep in mind that I have family who will be attending, as does Helen. These family members aren't quite as easygoing and casual as you and Zak. They'll be expecting a catered meal, not potluck. The dress you choose to wear will be discussed on all the society pages, as will the flowers you select and the music played."

"I'm getting married in less than two weeks," I pointed out. "I really don't think there's time to change everything I've already put in place."

"Between the two of us we can make a few minor adjustments," Mom assured me. "I'm sure you'll want to have a wedding you'll always remember."

"Oh, I'll remember it all right," I grumbled.

"Why don't you give Helen and me a day or two to see what we can come up with? With Pierre's help we're certain we can put together something everyone will love. When we've come to some decisions we can have another chat," Mom said.

I stood up. "Very well, but remember, this is *my* wedding. Scooter and Charlie are going to be the ring bearers and Alex and Bella are going to be the flower girls. Ellie will be the maid of honor and Levi will be the best man."

Both moms opened their mouths.

"Nonnegotiable," I added before walking away.

Charlie and I were almost in tears after our encounter with the moms, so we decided to forget about my disaster of a wedding for the time being and focus on something else. I'd been meaning to head out to the lumberyard to try once again to catch the pregnant feline I'd been trying to trap for the past two weeks. The feral cat was cagey and seemed to be perfectly able to take care of herself, but I knew that when kittens were born in the wild it was very hard to domesticate them. And the chance of long-term survival for such kittens was slim. Not only did we have hard winters, with snow and subfreezing temperatures to deal with, but we had a large coyote population that considered the cats and kittens in the area to be nothing more than tasty treats.

I pulled into the lumberyard, which had been deserted since the previous December, when the office burned to the ground. I left Charlie in the truck when I climbed out and began my search. I'd seen the longhaired orange tabby hanging around the pile of lumber nearest the parking area on more than one occasion. I'd tried trapping her, but the old gal was smart. She seemed to know that the food I'd left for her was a trap and avoided it entirely.

"Here kitty, kitty," I called. I knew there was virtually no chance that she'd respond to my call, but it was a place to start. "I've come to take you to a warm, safe place to have your babies."

I stood quietly and waited. On the past occasions when I'd come by, the expectant mother had been curious enough to come out of hiding to check me out. In fact, with each visit she had come a tiny bit closer to allowing me to pet her. Today, however, there appeared to be no sign of her. I walked around the woodpile and tried to peer into the interior of the stacked lumber through the small openings. I didn't see anything and was about to leave when I heard a rustling. I turned around to find a pair of coyotes watching me from the edge of the forest.

"Shoo," I yelled.

The coyotes just looked at me.

I knew if the pair waited long enough they'd eventually catch up with the mother cat. I paused as I considered my next move. There was no way I was simply going to give up and leave the pregnant cat to the wild dogs. The fact that the mama cat hadn't shown herself could be due to the presence of the coyotes, or it could be because she was delivering or had recently delivered her kittens. The woodpile where I'd most recently seen her didn't seem like the best place to deliver. If I were a cat I'd choose somewhere a bit more sheltered.

I looked around the property, trying to think like a cat. Maybe she'd crawled under one of the sheds that lined the rear of the property. I glanced back toward the woods. The coyotes had retreated, at least for now. I grabbed one of my cat traps and headed toward the row of sheds. I got down on my hands and knees and looked under each one. I finally found the mama under the second to the last one I searched. She was curled up toward the middle of the shed and didn't seem at all inclined to come out.

There was no way I was going to fit under the shed, and it was impossible to move it, so I really had no way to get to the cat unless I could get her to come to me. I lay down on my stomach and attempted to make eye contact with the furry feline.

"Hey there. Remember me?" I asked in a soft, soothing voice. "I'm here to take you to a safe place to have your babies."

The cat didn't come any closer, but she didn't flee either. Maybe my persistence in visiting was going to pay off after all.

"So how about it?" I asked. "Are you going to come with me today?"

The cat meowed.

I tried to inch closer, but I couldn't squeeze into the small space.

The coyotes howled in the distance.

The cat inched closer to my outstretched hand.

"You know taking a chance with me is a better option than taking one that your canine visitors will go away and leave you alone."

The cat meowed again. I had the feeling we were communicating.

"I have salmon treats in the truck."

The cat inched toward me once again. She was less than four inches from my outstretched arm but still too far away to grab. I pulled my arm back a bit. I needed to lure her out before I made my move. If I grabbed for her and missed she might run right into the jaws of the carnivores waiting at the edge of the woods.

I kept talking to her and she continued to inch forward. Each time she came forward I retreated just a bit. It took a while, but eventually she was close enough to the edge of the building where I felt confident I could grab her if she would let me touch her. I slowly reached out a hand, talking to her the entire time. She'd never let me touch her before, but my guess was that she was already in labor. Perhaps she knew I wanted to help her because she remained in place as I grabbed her by the scruff of her neck and pulled her into my arms.

I could see the coyotes at the edge of the forest, watching me. "Sorry, guys," I said as I worked the cat into the cage I'd brought. "You'll have to find your dinner elsewhere."

By the time we arrived at the Zoo the cat was on the verge of delivering the first of her four kittens. Jeremy and I settled her into the birthing room and then watched from a distance in case she required assistance.

"It looks like you got to her just in time," Jeremy commented as she licked the first kitten clean.

"Yeah. I think she was almost glad to see me. There were a pair of coyotes lurking around, just waiting for her to come out from under that shed."

"She'll be safe here and the kittens will go to good homes. Who knows, maybe we can even find a home for Mama."

"I see we have a new litter of puppies." When I'd come in I'd noticed admittance paperwork for four lab mix puppies on the counter.

"Yeah. They're only five weeks old, but the lady who dropped them off insisted that she'd had enough of them and wasn't willing to keep them even another week. I'm supplementing their food with puppy formula."

"Did you talk to her about having Mama spayed?" I asked.

"I did. She said she couldn't afford it, so I gave her one of our vouchers."

One of the programs Zoe's Zoo offers was free or discounted spay and neuter service to pet owners who couldn't afford to pay for the procedure. Local veterinarian Scott Walden worked with us, accepting our vouchers as payment for services rendered. We compensated him for the vouchers he accepted at the end of each month.

"It seems like we have a bumper crop of puppies this year," I commented.

"It does seem like our canine population is more fertile than usual. Maybe we should rerun the ad we had in the paper last year offering the free and discounted spays and neuters. Could be that folks have forgotten about it."

"That's a good idea. Just use the ad we had last year. I'm going to head out. I need to go home to change before I meet up with Ellie and Levi for dinner. I'll see you tomorrow."

"Okay, boss."

"Oh," I turned back to Jeremy, "be sure that whoever is working the graveyard shift knows to look in on the kittens. I'm sure they'll be fine, but I like to keep a close eye the first twenty-four hours."

"Will do. Have a good dinner."

Charlie and I stopped at casa Zimmerman to get cleaned up before heading to the boathouse. I really hoped my mom was gone and that I wouldn't run into Mother Zimmerman. I wasn't at all happy that the two women had decided to team up. On the surface it appeared a better solution than bloodshed, but while I may have had a chance of getting to make at least some of the decisions if I tackled the moms one at a time, together they were a force I doubted anyone alive could reckon with.

Today it seemed luck was on my side. No one was around when I arrived at the house. I snuck upstairs, showered, and put on a clean pair of jeans and a tank top. I grabbed a sweatshirt for after the sun went down. Just as I was leaving the room I noticed the itinerary Mother Zimmerman had left for me. I could see she had quite successfully scheduled every moment of the week leading up to the wedding. The problem was that there wasn't a single activity I would even remotely enjoy.

"Maybe I should just call the whole thing off," I complained to my two best friends as soon as I arrived at the boathouse. I'd filled them in on the fact that the moms seemed to be ganging up on me and I felt helpless to fight them both.

"You're marrying Zak, not his mother, and your mom will calm down after the wedding," Levi said. "You love Zak. You want to be his wife. Don't let them ruin this for you."

"I'm pretty sure they already have."

"Here's what I'd like to suggest," Ellie spoke up. "Give the moms the day or two they asked for and then hear what they have to say. In the end, they can't make you do anything you don't want to. It's your wedding, and I know Zak will support any decisions you make."

The way things had been going I really doubted that, but I didn't say as much.

"And in the meantime?" I asked.

"Forget about it. Take a vacation from the wedding and focus on something else," Ellie said.

"Like the fact that Zak is going to break up with me?"

"Zak is *not* going to break up with you," Ellie insisted. "Why would you even think that?"

I explained about our conversation of the previous evening, and the less than desirable end result.

"Ouch. Zak's mom really is bulldozing you," Levi agreed. "If you want my opinion, Zak was just feeling you out to get a sense of how you would react to a change in plans. In the end he'll take your side and you'll get the honeymoon you planned."

"I wish I could believe you. I called and left a message for him this morning and he hasn't called me back. It's not like him to wait so long to call."

Neither Levi nor Ellie said anything. I could see they agreed with my assessment that it was odd that I hadn't heard back from Zak. He was normally very prompt about returning my calls. I was the one who tended to forget to check my messages. I took out my phone and glanced at it just to be sure Zak hadn't called and I'd missed it. He hadn't.

"They broke ground on the new strip mall outside of town," Levi offered.

I just looked at him.

He shrugged. "Ellie suggested you focus on something other than your wedding plans. I noticed today that they'd begun clearing the land for the strip mall they've been trying to build for the past two years and I figured I'd mention it."

"I still can't believe the town council approved that project," I complained. "Everyone knows it's going to distract from Ashton Fall's small-town feel."

"From what I hear, the council only approved the project after the developer agreed to give the building a woodsy appearance," Ellie added.

"It won't help," I argued. "All the wood siding in the world isn't going to cover the fact that Ashton Fall's has opened its doors to allow retail chains to operate in the area. My dad thinks that once the strip mall opens a lot of local businesses are going to go under."

"Is he concerned about Donovan's?" Ellie asked.

"He says he's not unconcerned. On one hand, my mom has a lot of money, so my parents will be fine financially no matter what happens. On the other, Donovan's has been a family-owned and -operated business in Ashton Falls for two generations. My dad loves that store. It's going to kill him if the retail chains that eventually populate the mall put him out of business."

"You know what's odd," Levi said, "I attended the council meeting when the developer first introduced the idea of the mall. One hundred percent of the council members were firmly against it. Now all of a sudden the project is approved and under construction. I have to ask myself what changed."

"It's been two years," Ellie pointed out. "Maybe the developer was persistent and managed to wear down enough of the council to get the approval."

"Yeah, maybe." Levi still didn't seem convinced.

"I've seen it happen," I agreed with Ellie. "Sometimes it's the one who commits to relentless perusal of what they want that wins in the end. Which reminds me that I should head home and try to call Zak again. I have a feeling groveling might be the order of the day."

"Let's get together for lunch tomorrow," Ellie suggested. "We can all head to the Beach Hut after the meeting."

Levi, Ellie, Zak, and I are all members of the Ashton Falls Events Committee. Although the annual Fourth of July celebration was barely in the rearview mirror, the committee was already looking ahead to the Haunted Hamlet weekend in October.

"I can't believe we're already going to start talking about Halloween," I muttered.

"The Haunted Hamlet is a big event, and the committee wants to expand it even more," Ellie reminded me. "I just hope they don't ask me to chair it. I feel like I already have my hands full."

I let my thoughts wander to Halloween. By the time the event rolled around, Zak and I would be married and this whole wedding nightmare would be well behind us. I just hoped I could make it through the next couple of weeks without killing someone in the process.

Chapter 5

Tuesday, July 14

The weekly events committee meeting was held in the back room of Rosie's Café. The chairperson for the committee, Willa Walton, called the meeting to order shortly after I sat down. I had intentionally shown up just a few minutes late so as to avoid the inevitable wedding questions that had been plaguing me of late.

"So, less than two weeks until the big day," Willa began.

Damn.

"I hear you brought in a wedding planner," Hazel Hampton added.

"Mrs. Zimmerman has hired a wedding planner," I clarified. I smiled at Hazel, despite the fact that I really didn't appreciate her bringing up the situation.

"Personally, I don't think we need anyone to do what I've already done, but whatever. We're here to discuss the Haunted Hamlet," I said, attempting to change the subject.

"I overheard some women at the Clip and Curl discussing the photo shoot," Tawny Upton added. "*Modern Day Celebrities*; now that's really something. I wasn't going to buy a new dress for the wedding but there might be photos of the crowd."

Tawny was a single mother, and I knew she was likely to use any social event that might lead to dating opportunities to her advantage.

"I'm not sure we've absolutely decided to let the magazine do the article," I said. There was no way I wanted to spend the day avoiding the cameras I just knew were going to capture any and all embarrassing moments. I'd read the magazine. They seemed to get a certain satisfaction in catching the bride in oops moments.

"Now as for the Haunted Hamlet," I continued, "I was thinking that maybe we should start looking for a new location for the haunted barn. Newton Potter was moved to a care facility a few months ago. He has an old barn on his property, so maybe if we approach him now . . ."

"Do you think any actual celebrities might show up now that *Modern Day Celebrities* is covering the wedding?" Gilda Reynolds, owner of Bears and Beavers and community theater leader, asked.

Were these people even listening to what I was saying?

"Like I said," I answered, "I'm pretty sure the magazine is out."

I had managed to express my concern to my mom, and she didn't disagree that having the magazine there was a bad idea. She said she'd talk to Zak's mom about it.

"Now about the Potter barn . . ." I attempted to bring the conversation back around to the subject we were gathered to discuss. "It's actually a pretty large structure, and although it hasn't been used to house livestock in a couple of decades, it's in pretty good shape."

"I read in one of those gossip magazines that celebrities sometimes seek out invitations to events where they might be photographed by the right people," Willa informed the committee members.

I looked at Levi, who grinned and shrugged. Leave it to my *ex*-best friend to be taking pleasure in my obvious discomfort. If Ellie were there she'd bail me out, but Kelly was sick, so she had to cover at the Beach Hut and wasn't able to attend the meeting. Levi and I were joining her after the meeting for the lunch we'd planned.

"Zoe makes a good point about the barn." My dad finally spoke up. "If we wait too long we're going to have to scramble to find something. I think we should have someone talk to Newton."

"I nominate Zoe." Tawny raised her hand. "It was, after all, her idea."

"Usually the event chairperson is in charge of securing a facility," I reminded the group.

"I nominate Zoe to be event chairperson," Tawny added. "I wonder if it's inappropriate to wear red to a wedding. I have a red dress that I bought for a date last Valentine's Day that will definitely make a statement."

"I was chairperson for the winter carnival," I reminded the group. Normally, we all took turns so as not to create too much of a burden on any one person.

"And you did a wonderful job," Willa commented. "Do I have a second?"

"I second," Levi said.

I kicked him in the shin. Hard.

"Maybe we should mix it up a bit." My dad attempted a rescue.

"We need to vote on the motion on the table," Willa reminded him. "It's been made and seconded.

All in favor of Zoe serving as chairperson for Haunted Hamlet?"

"Aye," everyone except my dad responded.

"All opposed?" Willa asked.

My dad looked at me and shrugged.

"Okay, the motion is carried," Willa announced. "Congratulations, Zoe, you are the official Haunted Hamlet chairperson for this year. So about the food . . ."

"For the Hamlet?" I asked.

"No, the wedding. Surely now that you have a celebrity wedding planner you're going to ditch the idea of a buffet. I've always thought salmon to be a good choice for a daytime wedding."

"I thought you liked the idea of a buffet," I reminded her.

"I did when it was just going to be a small, casual affair. But if there are going to be celebrities in attendance, a sit-down meal served by wait staff is a must."

"Maybe Dirk Pendleton will come," Gilda suggested. "You know he has a house in the area."

Dirk Pendleton wasn't only a movie star, he was a *huge* movie star. This conversation was getting ridiculous.

"I think we may need to rethink the flowers for the tables," Hazel said. "I'm thinking about orchids now."

It was at that point that I checked out. Not literally. I politely stayed while the committee discussed my wedding like it was any other community event that needed to be haggled over. What is it about weddings that brings out the worst in people?

After the meeting Levi and I headed to the Beach Hut. It wasn't quite lunchtime yet, so the midday rush had yet to arrive. Ellie made sandwiches for the three of us to eat out on the deck. It was another perfect day in paradise. The sun was shining, the birds were singing, and the lake was perfectly calm and deeply blue. On most days such as this I would have been walking around with a song in my heart and a skip in my step, but today I was simply miserable.

"Did you ever get hold of Zak?" Ellie asked.

"Sort of. I called him when I got home last night. He was polite but distant. He sounded tired. I didn't bring up the honeymoon fiasco and neither did he. Our conversation was short. He told me that he was right in the middle of writing the new code and really needed to finish, but I sensed there was something more to it."

"Maybe Zak will work something out with his mom," Levi offered.

"Maybe." I sighed. "Even if he won't do it for me, I know he won't want to disappoint the kids."

"It does sound like a fun trip," Ellie agreed.

"You guys should come," I said. "I know you have some big decisions to make, but we'll only be gone for ten days and it'll be a lot of fun."

Ellie looked at Levi. I could see that she wanted to come along but was waiting for a cue from him.

"Would Kelly be able to handle things on her own?" Levi asked.

Ellie hesitated. "I'm not sure. I haven't brought this up before because I didn't feel like it was my place to do so, but I think Kelly's boyfriend has been hitting her."

"Hitting her?" I responded. "Did she tell you as much?"

"No, but I noticed she had a bruise on her cheek a few months ago. She'd tried to cover it up with makeup, but I could still see the faint discoloring. I asked her about it and she laughed and said she was such a klutz that she ran into an open cabinet door. I was pretty sure she was lying, but she changed the subject so quickly, I didn't want to push. Then two weeks ago she had on a long-sleeved shirt even though it was eighty degrees that day. I asked her if she was hot. She said she wasn't, but how could she not be? Later that day she pushed up her sleeves. I think it was an automatic response, and she pulled her sleeves back down right away, but not before I noticed there were bruises up and down both of her arms. And these are just the bruises I've been able to see. She never wears shorts, so who knows what she's covering up."

"Wow. Maybe you *should* talk to her," I said.

"I did. Sort of. After we closed the day I'd seen the bruises on her arm I pulled her aside and asked if I could help. She was very defensive and told me that everything was fine and she had things handled. When I suggested that it looked as if someone was hitting her, she told me it was none of my business and that I was her boss, not her mother."

"Ouch." I cringed.

"Ouch is right. She apologized the next day. She said she was out of line and she really did think of me as a friend, but she preferred to handle her personal life on her own."

"It's common for battered women to cover up what's happening," Levi reminded us.

"I know, but I'm really worried about her." Ellie sighed. "She called in sick today, but she sounded really odd. If I had to guess, there was someone else in the room listening to her conversation. Her words seemed almost rehearsed, and she got off the phone as quickly as she could. When I tried to call her later to check on her, she didn't answer the phone."

"I'll go by to check on her," Levi offered.

"No, I'll do it," I countered. "She would be more likely to talk to another woman. Maybe she really is sick. Either way, it gives me an excuse to delay calling Zak. I have a feeling our next conversation is going to conclude in a fight."

"Don't worry." Ellie squeezed my hand in support. "I'm sure Zak will side with you in the end."

"I hope so. I have to be honest: At this point I just hope we get through the wedding without any irreparable damage to our relationship."

"Remind me to elope when the time comes," Levi commented.

"You aren't serious," Ellie said firmly.

"After having a ringside seat at Zoe's fiasco I'm dead serious. How many people are staying at the house anyway?" Levi asked.

I began to count off the uninvited guests—at least uninvited by me—as I listed them. "For one, there's Mrs. Zimmerman. She invited three of Zak's cousins: Jimmy, Eric, and Darlene. Eric brought his wife Cindy, so there are currently five members of the Zimmerman family in the house. And I'm pretty sure additional relatives are on the way.

"In addition to the family," I continued, "there's the wedding planner, Pierre Bordeau, as well as his two assistants, Julianna and Longines. There's also a younger woman named Tasha, who seems to be an intern of sorts. Oh, and let's not forget Nikki Nicholson. She works for *Modern Day Celebrities* and has come to Ashton Falls early to write the backstory of our fairy-tale romance, which apparently is all about me because Zak isn't available."

"Yikes," Ellie sympathized.

"Yikes is right. The house is filled to the brim with people I don't even know and, quite frankly, don't want to know. I hate to side with Levi, but right now I totally agree with him. If I'd had any idea that my simple wedding would turn into this circus I would have eloped to Vegas."

"You just need to get through the next eleven days and it'll all be over," Ellie said encouragingly.

I looked out over the tourist-filled beach and wished with all my heart that I was among the crowd, who appeared to be enjoying the crystal-clear lake, white sand beach, and bright sunshine. If this were any other summer I would probably be out wakeboarding with Zak, Levi, and Ellie. We'd share a picnic on the beach and then maybe retire at the end of the day to the house for a BBQ and swim in the heated pool.

"By the way, I meant to tell you that I met Julianna this morning," Ellie volunteered. "She came in for coffee. She was with that reporter I told you about. The woman named Bridget. I'm sure she didn't realize I recognized her, but after you told us about Pierre's crew the other night I Googled them."

"Do you think she's feeding information to this woman?" I asked. "*Modern Day Celebrities* has an exclusive, at least until I can figure out a way to get rid of them. Neither Pierre nor Mrs. Zimmerman will be happy if someone scoops them. Of course if they get scooped maybe they'll all go away."

"They sat outside on the deck and I couldn't really linger without being obvious, but I watched them through the window. Julianna gave Bridget an envelope. I couldn't tell what was inside, but I did overhear Julianna say they were even now. Even for what, I don't know. I suppose Julianna could have owed Bridget some sort of debt. The thing is that Bridget didn't seem to agree with Julianna's assessment of the situation. I couldn't hear everything that was said, but it seemed like Bridget felt Julianna still needed to do something more before they were indeed even."

"Great. Just what I need. A blackmail conspiracy of unknown origin right in the middle of my disaster of a wedding. Julianna might be leaking photos and inside facts, like times and dates. Guest lists. That sort of thing. My wedding is going to become a media circus on the cover of every rag out there."

"The conversation could have been about something else," Ellie offered.

"Yeah, maybe Julianna is selling government secrets like Claudia Lotherman was," Levi teased.

Claudia Lotherman was a spy who made her living selling government secrets to the highest bidder. I'd run into her in Alaska the previous December and almost died as a result of our encounter. I'd managed to swim my way to safety, but Claudia got away. Somehow I doubted Julianna was a spy as well, but she very well could be selling software secrets. I filled Levi and Ellie in on the details of the office break-ins.

Levi frowned. "I was just joking around to lighten the mood, but you could be on to something. Maybe Julianna's been the one sneaking around in Zak's office."

"Yeah, but why?" Ellie asked. "I'm sure Zak's important papers are locked up."

"I need to go back to the house to look around some more," I decided. "If someone *is* stealing information I need to alert Zak."

"I'll go with you," Levi offered. "Why don't you check on Kelly first, though? I'll wait here. Call me when you're done and I'll meet you at your house. We can look around to make sure everything is in order and then maybe take the dogs for a hike."

"Sounds good. I'll head over to Kelly's now."

Kelly lived in a small apartment less than a block from the Beach Hut. The complex was old and somewhat run-down, but the location made the two-story complex popular nonetheless. Kelly lived on the bottom floor of the structure.

I knew that if Kelly was the victim of domestic violence she would most likely be less than thrilled with my presence on her doorstep. Ellie had heated some chicken soup she'd had in the freezer, providing an excuse for my visit should I need one.

I'd met her boyfriend on a couple of occasions. He'd seemed friendly enough, but now that I considered what Ellie had told me, I could see how he could be an abusive man. He was good-looking and a little arrogant, with a rehearsed charm that seemed authentic on the surface but didn't quite stand up to deeper scrutiny. I remembered he'd had a hard time holding a job. He seemed to start off okay, but his temper usually managed to get him fired before too much time passed.

When I arrived at the apartment the blinds were drawn across the front window. I knocked on the door and waited. I could hear a rustling inside, but no one came to the door. I knocked again.

"Kelly, are you home?" I called. "It's Zoe. Ellie sent me with soup."

I noticed the blinds moving just a bit.

"It's chicken and rice. She said it's your favorite."

"I'm not really up to having visitors at the moment," Kelly called back through the door.

"No problem. I can't stay anyway. I just wanted to drop off the soup. Maybe I can just pass it in."

"I'm not really very hungry," she tried.

"I understand, but you might be later. It smells really good. You could always just stick it in the refrigerator and then reheat it when you're feeling better."

Kelly opened the door a crack. She reached out an arm that was covered in a long-sleeved shirt, even though it was in the mideighties. I handed her the paper bag. She quickly pulled it inside and closed the door again.

"Are you sure you're okay? Do you need anything? I can run to the store if you need me to."

"I'm fine. It's just a nasty flu." Kelly spoke through the closed door. "Tell Ellie I'll call her later. I'm pretty sick. I'll probably miss a couple of days"

"Okay, I'll tell her. And Kelly . . . if you need anything at all, day or night, please don't hesitate to call."

"Thank you. I appreciate that. But I'm fine, really. Like I said, it's just a nasty flu."

I very much doubted it was the flu keeping Kelly at home, but it wasn't my place to point out that I suspected she was lying.

I called Levi when I got back to my truck and told him to meet me at the house. I was worried about Kelly, but I'd done all I could. She was going to have to ask for help if she was going to escape her jerk of a boyfriend. If and when she came to that point, she had good friends who would be there to help her through whatever was going on.

When I got to the house Julianna was nowhere in sight. I ran into Longines, who told me that Mother Zimmerman and Pierre were off on some errand that promised to keep them occupied most of the day. I didn't see any sign of Jimmy, Tasha, Nikki, or the other cousins, which meant that Longines was the only guest currently on the premises. I made up a fake errand for the flamboyant man, which left Levi and me alone to snoop around undetected.

Part of the problem was that I didn't know exactly what it was I was looking for. Levi and I went through the folders clearly visible on Zak's desk, but I doubted he would leave anything worth stealing in plain sight. There was a safe behind the bookshelf that slid to the side when a secret lever was accessed. Even I didn't have the combination, but Levi helped me move the bookcase so we could confirm that the safe was securely locked. We opened and closed drawers, but nothing jumped out as having been disturbed.

"Maybe you should call Zak to fill him in," Levi counseled. "We don't know what we're looking for, and it stands to reason that if something's missing we probably wouldn't even realize it. The lock on the door is a good one, and the door isn't damaged, so if someone did break in they knew what they were doing. If they have that level of expertise in breaking and entering they most likely aren't going to leave obvious clues."

"Yeah, I guess you're right. I'll call him later this evening, when he's less likely to be in the middle of work."

I got up from the spot on the floor where I'd been examining the bookshelf and looked around the room. Everything appeared to be in order. I was heading toward the door when Levi bent over and picked up a button from the floor.

"This belong to you?"

I took it from him for a closer look. It was dark blue, in the shape of a triangle. "It's not mine, and I don't recognize it as being Zak's. Of course he does have a lot of shirts, so I guess it could be his, but it's kind of an odd shape for a button on a dress shirt."

"We should hang on to it. It might prove to be a clue if we decide that someone has broken in," Levi said.

I put the button in my pocket before Levi and I exited the room. I locked the door behind us.

"Ready for that hike?" Levi asked.

"Boy   am   I."

Chapter 6

"Do you mind stopping by Newton Potter's place?" I asked Levi as we headed out of town toward the trailhead of the hike we planned to take. "Now that I've been railroaded into chairing the Haunted Hamlet and securing a location for the haunted barn, I'd like to get a head start on the process."

"I thought you planned to talk to Potter to ask him if we can use the barn."

"I do. It's just that I sort of brought the barn up as a desperate means of diverting attention from all the wedding talk. I really should take another look at it before I track him down."

"I guess I should apologize for seconding Tawny's nomination."

"It really was pretty rotten of you, but you can make it up to me by acting as my co-chair."

"I'm not sure I'll even be here in October."

"So you're really thinking about taking that job?"

"Yeah. I really am," Levi said. "It's an awesome opportunity I may never have again. I don't want to move, but I don't see how I can pass it up either."

The idea of Levi leaving was just too depressing to deal with, so I changed the subject.

"I don't suppose you know anything about the death of that homeless guy a few years back in Potter's barn?" I asked.

"No. I haven't heard anything since it happened," Levi confirmed as he pulled off the highway onto the ranch road.

"I remember the body was found, and it was determined he froze to death because there didn't seem to be any trauma involved. It was before Potter moved, and he reported that he hadn't heard or seen anything."

"I guess that sort of thing could happen."

"I guess. I just can't help but think about the drifters who appeared to have been scared to death in Hezekiah Henderson's old house. It just got me thinking about the history of this place."

"It might not hurt to do a search. The property is old. There must have been at least a couple of owners before old Potter. Who knows what sort of creepy things might have happened there in the past."

"A search might be a good idea."

Levi turned onto the private drive and pulled up in front of the deserted house. The property was about five miles outside of town, close enough that folks wouldn't mind making the drive to visit the attraction, but far enough away that it provided a spooky feel to the place. It would be easy enough to decorate the drive leading to the house with skeletons, tombstones, and other teasers to get the guests in the spirit of the event.

Levi parked and we got out and headed toward the slightly dilapidated barn. It was two-storied, with a hayloft at the top. The interior of the dusty structure was divided into individual stalls that could be converted into minirooms with the help of temporary walls.

"It has promise," I stated.

"I like the overall feel of the place," Levi agreed. "Now that Joel is out of the picture, have you thought about who you're going to get to transform this place into a barn of terror?"

"I haven't gotten that far yet." Joel Ringer had been the mastermind behind the haunted barn for years before we discovered he was actually a homicidal maniac. He'd managed to escape, but due to his fugitive status, I doubted he was going to be available to help out this year.

"You might try talking to the drama department at the high school. They did a good job with the haunted hayride last year."

There was a crashing sound that seemed to come from overhead.

"What was that?" I asked.

"I have no idea."

"It seemed to be coming from up there." I looked up toward the loft.

Levi looked overhead. "Maybe something just shifted. I suppose that happens at times with old buildings."

"Or maybe the whole thing is about to come crashing down on us." I heard a loud groan.

"It seems to be pretty solid. Hang on while I climb up there to take a look."

"Be careful. I have a funny feeling about this."

I waited while Levi climbed the rope ladder to the overhead room. I could hear him walking around. The building was drafty, but we could warn folks to dress warm. Then I heard a fluttering coming from the rafters. I almost screamed when I spotted the bats. If they decided to hang around they would definitely lend to the spooky atmosphere.

"It seems solid enough, but it looks like there's blood up here," Levi called down. "It could be animal blood, but you might want to check to make sure that drifter really did die from exposure and not a hit on the head."

"I distinctly remember the newspaper saying he froze to death. You don't think more than one person has died in here, do you?"

"Probably not."

I heard another crash.

"What was that? Are you okay?" I could see the edge of the loft, but I could no longer see Levi, who must have moved toward the back wall.

"I'm fine. There was a pitchfork leaning on the wall. It fell right in front of me and almost hit me in the head. Maybe there *are* ghosts in here."

Terrific. Leave it to me to suggest an actual haunted barn for the annual event.

"How about we get out of here?" I suggested. "I'll call Potter and get the history of the place before we make a firm decision to use it or not."

Levi climbed back down the ladder. "You wanted spooky. This place is definitely spooky. If you think about it, an actual legend about a ghost on the property would lend itself to an extrascary event. It could really work for us."

"Unless the legend isn't a legend and there's a real ghost," I pointed out. "You did say the pitchfork tried to kill you."

"I said no such thing. I said it fell and almost hit me in the head."

"Sounds like the same thing to me. Besides, you were the one who suggested there could be an actual ghost here."

"I was kidding."

I frowned as I looked around the barn.

"You're letting your imagination get the better of you," Levi said. "How about that hike? I bet the dogs are getting tired of waiting in the car."

It was late by the time Charlie and I got home, but judging by the number of lights on in the house the crew was still up and about. I didn't want to deal with Momzilla, Zak's cousins, or the wedding planner, so I decided to go around to the house to sneak in through the back door. Charlie and I made our way slowly around to the back of the house, keeping an eye out the whole time for anyone who might be lurking outdoors. We'd almost made it to the back door when we noticed someone in the pool. Zak's pool is the indoor/outdoor type, with a roof and walls that retract when the weather is nice. It was the middle of the summer, so the walls were retracted at the moment. The pool was heated, but it was a little nippy this late in the evening, so I was surprised that anyone would brave the chill to take a swim. I walked toward the side near the deep end to take a closer look. What I discovered upon closer examination was that the person I'd thought was swimming was actually floating, and unless I was mistaken, the person in the water was Pierre's assistant, Julianna, and she wasn't taking a swim, she was quite dead.

I dove into the pool just in case and pulled the body to the side of the pool to check for a pulse. I dragged the body to the shallow end, pulled it out of the water, retrieved my cell phone, which was, thankfully, encased in a waterproof case, and dialed 911.

By the time Sheriff Salinger arrived, I'd notified everyone who was still downstairs of Julianna's death and changed into dry clothes. Julianna had been fully clothed, and there was a cut on her head. There was a small amount of blood on the tile on the side of the pool. It appeared she'd either fallen into the pool, hitting her head as she entered the water, or she'd been pushed.

"Who *are* all these people?" Salinger asked me as soon as we were alone.

"The lady who's feigning a panic attack in the living room is Zak's mother. The others are either family members or part of the wedding planner's crew."

"I thought you told me that you wanted to have a small wedding."

"I did."

"I see." Salinger actually had sympathy in his eyes, which was a statement regarding how far our relationship had come, as far as I was concerned. "And Zak?"

"On the East Coast. He left before the circus showed up. Hopefully he'll be home in a few days."

"I take it you're less than thrilled by the arrival of the wedding guests and crew?" Salinger asked.

"Less than thrilled is putting it mildly. These people are like locusts. They seem to have spread to every room in the house."

"Did you kill the woman in the pool?"

I just glared at Salinger.

"You know I had to ask."

"No, I didn't kill her. I went hiking with Levi, and then I was over at the boathouse with him and Ellie right up until the time I found the body, if you're wondering about my alibi."

"Do you have any idea who might have killed her?" Salinger asked.

"I barely met her. She's the assistant of the wedding planner, a guy by the name of Pierre Bordeau."

"And how well do you know this Pierre Bordeau?"

"I don't know him at all. He's just some guy Zak's mom came up with. There is one thing, though." I filled Salinger in on the conversation Ellie had overheard between Julianna and the woman named Bridget.

"Can you describe this Bridget?"

"No. I've never seen her. Ellie has, though. Twice. She can probably give you a description."

"And you have no idea what was in the envelope Julianna gave her?"

"No. We talked about what it might be at lunch. I think it's most likely dirt from the wedding to spill to competitors, although we also entertained the notion that Julianna might have stolen something from Zak's office."

I explained about seeing the lights on and finding the files disturbed.

"I'm going to need to call Zak," Salinger informed me.

"I figured. I don't suppose you're going to ask everyone to leave now that the house is a crime scene?" I asked hopefully.

"Quite the opposite. I'm going to insist that everyone who's on the premises remain here until I can sort this out."

"I was afraid of that."

Later that evening, after Salinger had left and everyone else had settled into their respective rooms, I returned the 700 messages Zak had left on my phone since he'd spoken to Salinger. I'd like to think I was simply waiting to return his calls until I had a moment to myself, but if I was going to be totally honest, there was a small part of me that was getting him back for not returning my calls in a timely manner.

"Are you okay?" Zak asked.

I began to cry as soon as I heard the panic in his voice.

"I'm fine. I'm sorry I didn't get back to you sooner. Between Salinger and the house full of guests, I was tied up until now."

"God, Zoe, I was so worried."

"I know. I'm sorry." I found that I really was sorry.

I heard Zak let out a long breath. "No, *I'm* sorry. I never should have left you there alone with my mother. I knew she was going to do exactly what she's doing, and I never should have let it happen."

"I know you just did what you had to do. It's not like you could let your client's system get hacked."

"I know, but I should have handled my mother before I left. If I had, the wedding planner would never have been hired and this accident would never have happened."

"Actually, Salinger thinks it was an accident, but I'm not so sure," I answered.

I know you can't hear a frown, but I could swear I heard Zak frown.

"What do you mean, you aren't so sure?" Zak asked. "What do you think happened?"

"I think Julianna might have been pushed."

"Pushed? Who would push her?"

"Pierre, for one. He's the wedding planner your mom hired. Nikki, for another," I answered.

Zak let out a long breath. I could picture him rubbing his forehead with his fingertips.

"Who's Nikki?" Zak asked.

"A reporter."

"Maybe you'd better start at the beginning," Zak suggested.

"Pierre and his crew showed up on Sunday," I began. "I made it clear that the wedding was already planned and we didn't need a wedding planner, but that was when your mother announced that our plans would never do because she'd made a deal with *Modern Day Celebrities* to photograph the wedding."

"What?" Zak sounded genuinely surprised. "There's no way I want to spend my wedding day tripping over a bunch of reporters."

"My sentiments exactly."

"So this Nikki works for *Modern Day Celebrities*?"

"She does. She's here early to do a backstory on us."

"Wonderful." Zak sighed.

"I know; right? I've been avoiding her since she arrived, but I just know she's going to catch me in an awkward moment, snap a shot, and plaster it all over the tabloids."

Zak groaned. "Okay, so why would this Nikki want to kill Julianna?"

"Ellie saw Julianna give a woman we only know as Bridget an envelope," I began. "We suspect she's a reporter for a rival magazine."

"Wait. I'm confused. Is this Bridget staying at the house too?"

"No. Bridget showed up at the Beach Hut and asked questions about us. She wanted to know where we lived. Ellie didn't tell her anything, but she suspected the woman was a reporter, although she never actually admitted as much," I rambled. "She never showed up here, so I was hoping she'd given up and gone away, but then, earlier today, Ellie saw Julianna meet her at the restaurant. That was when Julianna gave Bridget the envelope."

Zak paused. I could sense he was confused by my explanation, although he's gotten a lot better at decoding my ramblings than he used to be.

"So you think Nikki pushed Julianna into the pool because she was leaking photos that would ruin her exclusive?" Zak eventually asked.

"Exactly."

"And Pierre?"

"I don't know this for certain, but it seems he only took this job because the magazine was going to shoot the wedding. I think he's linked with the magazine in some way, although I haven't had time to figure out the specifics. If I had to guess. I'd say he must get a cut of whatever the magazine makes off our photos. If Julianna gave photos to a rival magazine, any photos *Modern Day Celebrities* might come up with would be worth considerably less."

"So you think either Pierre or Nikki killed Julianna because she leaked photos to a rival magazine."

"Correct."

"I know there's a lot going on, and I know the circus my mom has created is causing you a lot of stress," Zak continued, "but I really doubt someone murdered this woman over a couple of photos, even if that was what was in the envelope."

"Yeah, I guess you're right. I've been pretty outraged ever since the wedding planner showed up, so that could be clouding my judgment, but I really feel there's more going on than a slip and fall."

Zak sighed again. "I'm really close to getting this hacker blocked once and for all. I hope to have things wrapped up tomorrow, and then I'll pick up the kids on Thursday. Do you think you can hang in there until then? We can figure this all out when I get home."

"I'll be fine," I assured him. "I just want us to have our house back."

"I'm not sure there's much I can do about that until I get home. Why don't you go stay with Ellie until then?"

I thought about telling him about the office break-in, but I didn't want to worry or distract him.

"No, I should stay here to keep an eye on things. I'll be fine," I promised.

"You know I love you. More than anything or anyone," Zak reminded me.

"I know. I love you too. More than anything or anyone. Well, maybe except for Charlie," I teased

Chapter 7

Wednesday, July 15

"So Salinger thinks she fell in the pool?" Jeremy asked me the next morning as we cleaned the animal cages.

I only planned to spend a couple of hours at the Zoo, so I'd left Charlie with Levi, who was going to take the dogs for a run. We'd arranged to meet up later in the afternoon.

"That's what he said. It seems there was no sign of a struggle, nor were there any defensive wounds on the body. Several of the other *uninvited guests* reported that Julianna had been drinking before she announced she was going out for some fresh air. Salinger believes she tripped, or perhaps slipped, on the damp concrete and fell into the pool, hitting her head on the way in. He believes she was knocked unconscious and then drowned. I, on the other hand, am not as sure it was an accident, but I have to admit I have no actual evidence to prove it. It's really strange, though. When I got up this morning things were pretty much back to normal. Everyone was going about their business, doing what they felt needed to be done. Not one person even mentioned Julianna."

"You're kidding?" Jeremy stated as we removed our tools and supplies from the enclosure.

"I wish I were. The whole thing is really sort of creepy. I mean, think about it: A woman who everyone knew and worked with has died and no one seems to even notice she isn't there. Other than the fact that Salinger has taped off the pool area, you'd never even know anything occurred."

"So if you don't think it was an accident, what do you think happened?" Jeremy asked as we finished up in the bear cage and then released the door to the holding cell so the cubs could wander back inside.

"I don't know for certain," I admitted. "I have no reason to think Julianna's death was anything but an accident, but in my experience just because something looks like an accident doesn't mean that's what it is. Besides, there's that whole thing with the envelope."

"What whole thing with what envelope?"

I filled Jeremy in on the conversation Ellie overheard and our suspicions as to what the envelope might contain.

"Has anyone spoken to this Bridget?" Jeremy asked.

"As of the last time I spoke to Salinger, he's had no luck tracking her down. Ellie never did catch a last name, and we really only speculated that she was a reporter. She could have been meeting with Juliana for another reason entirely."

"I assume you called Zak to let him know what happened," Jeremy added as we began to clean the cat room.

I bent down to pick up one of the kittens we'd recently rescued from a shelter in the valley. I held her to my chest, scratching her under the chin as I answered. "Yeah, I called him. He offered to come home right away, but I told him to go ahead and finish what he was doing. I think he's concerned that I'm going to nose around in the case."

"And are you? Going to nose around?"

I set the kitten back down on the floor. "Probably. I've been thinking about it. If Julianna was pushed, there are two possibilities: Either she was pushed by someone at the house who took advantage of the fact that she separated herself from the group in order to get some fresh air, or she was lured outside by someone who then killed her. The reality is that if the killer is someone who's staying at the house, once Zak gets home and kicks everyone out, the odds of proving what actually happened will be slim. He should be home on Friday, so I need to work fast if I want to bring Julianna's killer to justice, assuming there's a killer to find."

"Do you have any suspects?" Jeremy asked.

"Initially, I thought it was either the wedding planner or the reporter. Ellie and I think Julianna may have leaked photos to a rival magazine. But after speaking to Zak I've decided that might not be a strong enough reason to kill a person. I've decided to assume that everyone who was on the property is a suspect."

"It really does sound like she may have just tripped and fallen," Jeremy pointed out.

"Maybe. But I need a distraction from the wedding nightmare my life has become; I'm hoping investigating will provide enough of a distraction that I'll be able to avoid killing Zak's mom while I'm waiting for him to get home."

"Yeah, I guess *that* would put a damper on the wedding." Jeremy laughed. "You knew Zak when he lived here before. Was his mother always this intense?"

I thought back to the days when Zak was just a kid who went to my school, not a superstar software developer. He'd arrived in my life when I was in the seventh grade, and I'd hated him on sight. Well, maybe I didn't *hate* him, but he'd been a huge thorn in my side. My disdain for Zak began when he slaughtered me in a mathathon I'd been relentlessly studying for for almost three months in order to impress my maternal grandparents, a scary couple I'd met only a handful of times yet still inexplicably wanted to please. Zak not only massacred me but he'd done so, I later found out, without even studying.

"I didn't know Zak's mom well," I answered. "It's not like Zak and I hung out. But I don't remember her being quite so over the top. Chances are Zak's success has gone to her head. He tried to warn me that she would try to run things. In fact, we were engaged for several months before Zak even told his mom we were getting married. He wanted to be sure we had our own plans in place first. I guess that was all for naught."

Jeremy squeezed my shoulder in a show of comfort. "Don't worry. Zak said he'd fix things, and I'm sure he will."

Tiffany stuck her head in the door. "There's a woman here to see you, Zoe."

"Do you know who it is?"

"She said her name is Nikki Nicholson."

I frowned. Why would the reporter from *Modern Day Celebrities* come to the Zoo?

"Tell her I'll be right out."

After I finished what I was doing I washed my hands and headed toward the lobby. "Welcome to Zoe's Zoo," I said, plastering the friendliest smile on my face I could muster given the circumstances. "Can I help you with something?"

"I've been sent to Ashton Falls to cover your wedding, but I'm really more interested in what you do here. I was hoping you'd be willing to give me a tour, maybe let me take some photos of your facilities and the animals, and perhaps ask a few questions."

Suddenly my smile was real. "I'd love to. Why don't you come back to my office and we can chat for a few minutes. When Jeremy's finished cleaning the pens we can take a tour and you can get your photos."

"The whole reason I asked to cover your wedding was so I could get a look at your facility," Nikki admitted. "I think what you do to rescue and rehabilitate the animals in the area is totally awesome. Are there any wild animals on the premises at the moment?"

"We actually have a pretty full house. Not only is our bear cage filled to the brim with cubs who are too young to be on their own but we have a mountain lion cub and a pair of river otters as well. Oh, and then there are the assortment of squirrels, raccoons, and cottontail rabbits that seem to come in and out on a steady basis."

"Do you have different facilities for the wild and domestic animals?" Nikki wondered.

"We have different wings. The wild animals are down one hallway and the domestic animals are down the other."

"And your staff?" Nikki began to jot down notes.

"Jeremy Fisher is the facility manager. He's been with me since before the Zoo was the Zoo. Originally, we both worked for the county animal control shelter. When it was shut down Zak bought the facility and we opened Zoe's Zoo. I also have a full-time assistant, Tiffany Middleton, and two employees who work the graveyard shift, Tank and Gunnar Rivers. And we hire extra help in the summer, when we're the busiest."

I continued to answer Nikki's questions, and she had a ton of them. By the time Jeremy informed me he was finished cleaning the pens Nikki had a pad full of notes. She seemed friendly and enthusiastic, and it occurred to me that I might be able to get an insider's perspective of the events of the previous night.

"It's such a drag what happened to Julianna," I commented as we stood in front of the bear cage so Nikki could photograph the cubs.

"It really was a tragedy," Nikki agreed.

"Were you in the room when Julianna decided to go outside?" I asked.

Nikki lowered her camera and looked at me. "We all were at one point or another, although several of us did leave for a time."

"Such as?"

Nikki thought about it. "Eric and Cindy left after she caught her husband flirting with Tasha."

I remembered that Tasha was the intern I'd only spoken to on one occasion.

"I know the guy is your fiancé's cousin, but I have to say he's a real perv," Nikki continued. "He hit on me five minutes after we met, and I saw him in the hallway with Julianna on Monday evening. When I saw his wife slap him, all I could think was good for her. The guy is a snake."

"When did they leave the group downstairs?" I asked.

"I guess about fifteen minutes before Julianna went outside. Eric came downstairs later in the evening, but I never did see Cindy again until this morning."

"And when did Eric come back downstairs?"

"I think it was after Julianna went outside but before you found her."

I made a mental note to take a closer look at both Eric and Cindy. They'd both been absent from the main gathering when Julianna was pushed into the pool, and theoretically, they both had possible motives for pushing her. Cindy could have pushed her out of jealousy and Eric could have done it because she'd rejected his advances.

"Check out that little blond cub in the corner." Nikki raised her camera to her eye. "He seems so shy."

"He's a she, and she just came to us a few days ago. We're keeping her in isolation for her first couple of days here, so she's still getting used to being around the other cubs. I'm sure she'll be in the thick of things in a few days. So, other than Eric and Cindy, who else left the gathering?"

"Longines went upstairs early. Before Julianna went outside. He said he had a headache, and I don't remember seeing him again that night." Nikki bit her lip as she thought about it. "It kind of seemed like Tasha and Jimmy had a thing going on. They were hanging all over each other, and they left the gathering for at least half an hour. I think they left after Julianna went outside, but I can't swear to it."

I led Nikki down the hall to the large cat enclosure, where our mountain lion cub was hanging out. She snapped photos like crazy as we passed the pens where we kept the squirrels, raccoons, and other smaller animals. It was obvious she adored animals, and she seemed knowledgeable about them as well. It seemed a total waste that she was working for a celebrity magazine.

"What about Mrs. Zimmerman? Was she in attendance at the gathering for the entire time?" I asked as Nikki took shot after shot of the mountain lion cub, who'd decided to cooperate by coming out of his enclosure to play.

"No. Mrs. Zimmerman and Pierre spent most of the evening upstairs. They said they needed to go over their plans for the wedding."

"And what about Darlene?" I asked, mentioning another of Zak's cousins.

"She was downstairs the entire time. As a matter of fact, she and I talked for most of the night, or at least until you came in and told us Julianna was dead."

I tried to remember who was in the room when I went in after finding Julianna's body. Nikki and Darlene were in the room. I didn't remember seeing either Cindy or Longines, but I did remember seeing Eric.

It sounded to me like any of the guests could have snuck away to push Julianna into the pool. Nikki said she was with Darlene the entire time, so I supposed she had inadvertently given Darlene an alibi. I just needed to speak to Darlene to confirm that the two of them had been together, as Nikki indicated. She seemed the next person to interview. It would tell me a lot if her story paralleled or diverted from the accounting Nikki had just provided.

After Nikki left the Zoo, I decided to head back to the house to track down Darlene.

I found her stretched out on a lounge chair on the beach. She was alone, which was fortunate. Darlene was the youngest daughter of Helen Zimmerman's youngest brother, Joseph. At seventeen, she was the youngest cousin. Her older sister Twyla, mother of the progeny Helen thought were going to participate in the wedding as ring bearer and flower girl, was scheduled to arrive on the following Thursday.

It had taken me a while to sort out the Zimmerman cousins. I'd learned that including Zak, there were seven in all.

Jimmy, the eldest of the group, was thirty-six. He was the eldest son of Helen's older brother, Thomas. Jimmy had two younger brothers who planned to attend the wedding but weren't scheduled to arrive until the Friday before the event.

Eric was the only cousin who wasn't a Zimmerman. He was also the only cousin who was married. He was thirty-two. He'd married Cindy, who seemed to be close to his age, two years earlier. Based on the gossip I'd heard, I didn't know why he'd bothered to get married at all. He was the only child of Helen's younger sister, Wanda. Helen and Wanda had suffered a falling out years before and, according to what I'd learned from Cindy, Wanda didn't plan to attend the wedding.

"It's a beautiful day," I commented casually after sitting down on the lounger next to Darlene.

She shaded her eyes and looked over at me. "It's awesome. The perfect place to work on my tan. I didn't want to come to this stupid wedding at first, but now I'm glad I did. No offense."

I laughed. "None taken. I suppose spending two weeks out of the summer attending a cousin's wedding isn't exactly an ideal vacation."

"It certainly sounded like it was going to suck, but it's been pretty great so far. I had no idea nerdy Zak had such a nice place. I might have been out for a visit sooner."

"You're welcome any time," I told her.

"Can I bring my boyfriend?"

"Absolutely."

"You're okay. I really expected nerd boy to have an uptight, stuck-up fiancée, but you seem legit. And smart too, for clearing out and keeping your distance from the rest of those losers."

"You don't get along with your cousins?"

"Are you kidding? They're all pains in the ass, but Jimmy is the worst. He thinks he's the boss of everyone because he's the oldest, but he doesn't realize he's also the dumbest. All I can say is that it's a good thing he's good-looking; otherwise he'd have nothing going for him."

I couldn't help but chuckle. "And Eric?" I asked.

"Eric is seriously disturbed. The guy will hit on anything with an X chromosome. It's disgusting. I have no idea how he talked Cindy into marrying him. The only thing I can figure is that the prenup they signed guarantees her a pretty nice chunk of change if she stays with him for five years. I can see she's trying, but if you ask me, I doubt she'll make it that long without killing him."

"Do you get along with Cindy?"

Darlene shrugged. "Yeah. She's okay."

"And Jimmy's brothers?"

"Almost as dumb as Jimmy."

I looked out over the crystal-clear water as Darlene returned a text. It was a gorgeous day and I found all I really wanted to do was pour myself a cold drink and take a nap in the warm sunshine. But I had less than two days to solve a mystery, so sunbathing would have to wait.

"Sorry. It was Twyla," Darlene informed me. "She's all freaked out about bringing the kids out now that there's been a suspicious death."

"I guess I can't blame her for that."

"I wouldn't worry about it if I were her. Even a serial killer wouldn't want to be in the same room as her two brats."

"You don't get along with your niece and nephew?"

"I love my sister, but those two are the most annoying children on the planet. They're going to wreck your wedding."

"I already asked two other children to fill those positions," I informed Darlene. "Zak is picking them up on his way home. I told Mrs. Zimmerman as much, but she seems to be ignoring me."

Darlene laughed. "Sounds about right. You need to hold firm with her or she'll walk all over you. Trust me, bossing people around and getting her way is her superpower. Your best bet is to play up the murder angle, and then maybe Twyla and her irritating spawn won't come."

"That might be hard to do, considering the sheriff is calling the death an accident."

Darlene sat up. She adjusted the back of her chair and rolled over.

"I kind of doubt it was an accident," she replied. "I can think of four people off hand who had reasons to give Julianna a shove into the pool."

"Really? Who?"

"Aunt Helen, for one. I'm not sure how she managed to do it, but Julianna almost had Pierre convinced to bail on this wedding in favor of a new offer that came in from some guy who plays basketball for the Lakers. I can't remember his name; I'm not really a basketball fan."

I frowned. "Pierre was thinking about leaving before the wedding?"

"He would have, if Julianna had gotten her way. I overheard Aunt Helen and Julianna arguing. I guess Pierre doesn't even have a signed contract with her. Aunt Helen assured him Zak will sign the contract and pay the fee when he gets here, but Julianna didn't think so. She was pushing hard for them to dump this wedding in favor of the other one."

Darlene had just given me two valuable pieces of information. Not only was Helen Zimmerman suddenly a suspect but the contract I thought Zak was going to have to break didn't even exist.

"Do you remember where your aunt Helen was last night?"

"She was upstairs with Pierre for a while, but then she came down the back stairs, grabbed a bottle of wine that was sitting on the kitchen counter, and headed outside. She looked upset. Maybe Pierre was leaning toward doing what Julianna wanted."

I frowned. Nikki had said that she and Darlene were in the living room together the entire evening, so how could Darlene have witnessed Helen coming down the stairs and taking the wine? I decided to ask her.

"Nikki went to the bathroom, so I went into the kitchen to get a couple of beers," she answered. "Jimmy wouldn't let me have one while he was downstairs, but once he headed upstairs with Tasha I saw my chance and took it."

"So Jimmy and Tasha went upstairs just about the time your aunt Helen came down and went outside?"

"Yeah. I guess."

"You said there were four people who would want Julianna dead. Who else?"

Darlene leaned up onto her elbows and looked directly at me. I could see she was considering how much to say. The fact that she'd introduced the subject of suspects in the first place made it seem like she was willing to share their identities, but it appeared she might be having second thoughts.

"Eric was mad that Julianna blew him off when he tried to pick up on her, and Cindy was mad that Eric had managed to cop a feel before Julianna slapped him. I heard them arguing about it. Eric was trying to convince Cindy that Julianna came on to *him*. I doubt she was buying it, but then, she has three more years until her marriage is going to pay out. Maybe she tells herself what she needs to, to get by in the meantime."

"Nikki told me they had a fight and went upstairs, but then Eric came back down by himself."

"Yeah, that's how it seemed, but there *are* those back stairs. Other than going to the head, it seemed like Nikki was in the front of the house the entire evening. If Cindy came down the back stairs she wouldn't have seen her."

"And Eric?"

"He came back down at some point, but he was alone."

"Okay, so that gives us Helen, Cindy, and Eric as suspects. Who else?"

Darlene bit her lip, avoiding making eye contact with me. "I guess that's it," she finally replied. "I thought there might have been four, but I guess there were just three."

I could tell she was lying, but I let it go. She was obviously protecting someone, but given the fact that she didn't seem to like anyone, I couldn't imagine who it could be.

Chapter 8

I left Darlene and headed upstairs to check on the status of the office and the bedroom before heading out to meet Levi. While I still had no concrete evidence that someone had been snooping, I couldn't shake the feeling that both the office and the bedroom had been searched. I hadn't heard anything on the baby monitor, but I still believed it was possible that the rooms were being accessed whenever I was away from the house. If someone was breaking in to them the only explanation I could come up with was that someone was looking for notes or coding pertaining to Zak's new software program.

I thought about the people in the house and wondered who would try to steal something like that. Granted the information would be worth a lot of money, but in order to make anything off Zak's ideas, the thief would need to be smart enough to know what they were stealing *and* who to market it to.

Jimmy was the only houseguest I'd seen in Zak's office, but if Darlene was correct about his level of intelligence, I doubted he'd be able to find the safe, let alone get into it. Unless he was both smarter and more ambitious than he seemed, I doubted he was much of a threat.

Darlene only seemed to care about tanning and partying and Eric was a perv, but he had his own money, so I doubted he'd steal from Zak. Cindy likewise had a lot to lose if she was working toward a big divorce settlement. In spite of the fact that Zak's mom was making me nuts, I didn't see her as the type to steal from her own son, which left me with Pierre and his crew. None seemed like likely suspects off hand, but it wouldn't hurt, I decided, to keep an extraclose eye on everyone.

Pierre was an intelligent man with a lot of connections. It would actually be a brilliant idea to use wedding planning as a front to access the homes of the rich and famous and help yourself to the valuables contained within.

Longines had made himself scarce the entire time he'd been on the property. I thought he was going to be a pest, following me around in an effort to convince me to do a makeover, but other than the first day he'd arrived, I'd barely seen him. I supposed his absence made him a likely suspect.

I wasn't sure what to make of Tasha. She was young and seemed eager to do her job and do it well. She fluttered around much of the time, seeing to one task or another. I doubted she had the skill set to break into a locked office, locate and access a locked and alarmed safe, and steal software coding worth millions of dollars, but maybe . . . ?

I knew Zak was smart enough to keep his work encoded, so even if someone *did* find the files they were looking for, I doubted they'd be able to read them.

When I arrived at the top of the stairs I ran into Tasha, who was heading away from the hallway where Zak's office and our bedroom were located.

"Oh, good, there you are," Tasha greeted me as I waited at the top of the stairs. "Pierre wanted me to talk to you about setting up a time for you to meet with Longines."

"The wedding isn't for another ten days," I pointed out. "I hardly think it's necessary to start hair and makeup yet."

Tasha leaned in close and lowered her voice. "Between you and me, I agree. I think Pierre wants to do a trial run because Longines isn't his regular stylist."

"He's not?" I asked.

She shook her head. "The regular guy was in a car accident a few days before we were scheduled to leave for Ashton Falls. I'm not sure where Pierre found Longines, but as far as I know, this is their first time working together. I think Pierre just wants to make sure he knows what he's doing before the big day."

I frowned. I'd just assumed Longines had been with Pierre for the long haul. The fact that he was new to the crew made me wonder if his arrival hadn't been just a bit too convenient.

"How long have you worked with Pierre?" I asked.

"For about five months," Tasha answered. "He hired me as an unpaid intern with the promise of a full-time job when an opening came up."

"So now that Julianna is gone, this might be your shot?"

"I hope so," Tasha replied. "I've been waiting for Pierre to offer Julianna's position to me, but so far he hasn't said a word about a paid gig. Still, he may want to let things settle down a bit first. Julianna was with him a long time, so I'm sure a lot of his customers will be upset by her death."

"I imagine so."

"So about the meeting with Longines. Can you do it today?"

"I'm busy today. I'll find him later to arrange something," I promised.

"Okay, thanks," Tasha said before heading down the stairs.

As I watched her leave, I had to wonder if she really had been down the hallway of Zak and my private rooms looking for me or if she'd been snooping. The information that Longines was new to the group, and that Tasha had been working for five months waiting for a paid position to open up, vaulted both of them to the top of my suspect list. I had to ask myself if Tasha had become tired of waiting and created a job opening, or could Longines have orchestrated the accident of Pierre's regular stylist to gain access to this particular wedding party?

I decided I needed to share the new information I'd obtained with Salinger; plus I was interested in what the sheriff might have found out in regard to Bridget. I called Levi to tell him I was going to make a stop before I met him at the Beach Hut.

The sheriff's office in Ashton Falls is a satellite, housing a small staff. The main office in Bryton Lake handles most of the serious cases. Salinger has been trying to move to Bryton Lake his entire career, but so far he's been stuck in what I'm sure he considers to be a dead-end job. When we first met we didn't get along. At all. But as time has passed and I've helped him to solve a string of murders that's helped his career, we've settled in to a sort of unofficial partnership.

"Salinger in?" I asked the front-desk clerk.

"In his office. He saw you drive up and said to tell you to go on back."

I headed down the hall past the single holding cell. I hated to admit how often I'd made this trip during the past year and a half. I guess there are those who would say that my tendency to meddle is the root of the large number of near-death experiences I've suffered of late, but if you ask me, it's not so much that I go looking for trouble; it's more that trouble seems to come looking for me.

"Donovan," Salinger greeted me as I walked into the office and took a seat across from his desk.

"Salinger."

"Zak still out of town?"

"He is."

"So what can I help you with?"

"A couple of things. First off, I wanted to ask if you'd found out anything about the woman Ellie saw Julianna give the envelope to."

"Unfortunately, I haven't. Part of the problem is that we have very little to go on. We don't even know if her name is really Bridget. We don't have a photo of her or fingerprints, or any physical evidence, for that matter. I've checked all the local lodging facilities but none had a record of a Bridget registered at the time of the murder. I'm afraid at this point the Bridget lead is a dead end. I do have something new to share, however."

"Oh. And what is that?"

"The ME found a bruise on Julianna's arm that looks as if it was made by a narrow, cylindrical object."

"Like a bat?" I asked.

"Smaller. Maybe the handle of a golf club. If I had to guess I'd say someone tried to hit her and she put her arm up in self-defense. That may have been when she fell in the pool, or shortly before she fell."

"I thought there were no defensive wounds on the body."

"The bruise didn't show up right away. Based on this new evidence, I'm going to reclassify the drowning as murder rather than an accident. I'm not sure if that does us all that much good, but we now have access to additional resources if needed."

I found that I really liked the way Salinger used the term *we*. Trust me, it wasn't that long ago that he would have been threatening to lock me away for interfering.

"It seems like the killer has to be someone staying at the house," I said. "Did you get everyone's alibi when you spoke to them?"

"I did, although I wasn't calling them alibis at the time. Most of the guests covered for each other. There were a few individuals who appeared to have been alone during the death window." Salinger pulled out his notes.

"I spoke to Darlene earlier," I shared. "She told me that Longines went upstairs after complaining of a headache and stayed there the rest of the evening, and Eric and Cindy went upstairs after having a fight. Eric came back downstairs, but Cindy stayed upstairs."

"Yes, that's what I have as well. Helen Zimmerman was upstairs with Pierre and Jimmy, and Tasha Golding disappeared as well, leaving Darlene and Nikki Nicholson alone in the living room at the time Julianna went outdoors. It would seem on the surface that one of the two women killed Julianna, although both swear they were together the whole time."

"But they weren't," I informed Salinger. "Darlene told me that she went into the kitchen when Nikki went to the bathroom. She saw Helen come down the back stairs, grab a bottle of wine, and head out the back door."

"Are you saying you think Zak's mother killed the assistant to the wedding planner?"

"No, of course not," I answered. "I was just pointing out that *anyone* could have gone outside via the back staircase. If we assume that Julianna was killed by an individual acting alone and not a team, we need to ask ourselves who was alone for some period of time during the death window."

"Okay, so far I follow."

"At the time Helen left the house she was alone, which means Pierre was also alone because Helen is his alibi. If Darlene was in the kitchen she was alone for that short period of time, as was Nikki. And if Eric came downstairs after his argument with his wife, Cindy was also alone, as far as we know. I've given this some thought, and at this point it seems like everyone was alone at one point or another, so everyone could have done it."

Salinger sighed heavily. "That figures. I guess I should reinterview everyone now that we have additional evidence to try to put together a timeline."

"That might be a good idea. The pool is visible from the back door. If Mrs. Zimmerman went outside she would have noticed Julianna floating in the pool. One of two things must be true: Mother Zimmerman is our killer, which I really doubt, or our timeline is off."

"Assuming Helen Zimmerman isn't the killer, are you suggesting that the witnesses lied about the timing of Julianna's trip outdoors?"

"Maybe. The way it stands now, we know Julianna went outside for some air while several of the others were still in the living room. At some point after that, Jimmy went upstairs with Tasha, Nikki went to the bathroom, and Darlene went into the kitchen to try to sneak a beer. It was while she was in the kitchen that she saw her aunt Helen grab the wine and leave through the back door. After she secured the beer Darlene returned to the living room, Nikki came back from the bathroom, and Eric came back down from upstairs. Julianna had to have been outdoors for at least fifteen minutes by then. Maybe longer. If she was already in the pool Mrs. Zimmerman would have seen her. If Julianna was on the patio she would have been noticed as well."

"So either Helen Zimmerman did it or saw the victim in the pool but didn't say anything, or Julianna went somewhere before being pushed into the pool."

"It would seem," I agreed.

"I hate to say this, but Helen Zimmerman has already lied," Salinger pointed out. "When I asked about her whereabouts the night of Julianna's death she told me she was upstairs with Pierre. I have to say that I didn't ask her specifically if she was with him the entire time in that first interview, but she certainly didn't volunteer the information that she had left the house at all. I suppose reinterviewing her is as good a place as any to start."

"You might also take a close look at Tasha. I found out that she's been working as an unpaid intern for the past five months, waiting for a paid position to open up."

"And Julianna's death has provided just such an opening," Salinger concluded.

"Conveniently, yes. I also found out that Longines isn't Pierre's regular stylist. His usual guy was in an auto accident, so Longines is just filling in. Tasha thought it was his first time working with Pierre."

"Sounds like they're both worth taking a closer look at."

"Yeah." I nodded. "The thing is, I've come up with a motive of one type or another for almost everyone. I think new interviews are definitely in order."

I headed to the Beach Hut after I left Salinger's office. Just thinking about all the possible alibi and motive combinations was giving me a headache. Some time with my best friends was bound to make me feel better. I was tempted to call Zak and unload on him, but I knew he was working, and if all went well today, he'd be picking up the kids and heading home by tomorrow. The last thing I wanted to do was to interrupt him. Actually, I mentally corrected myself, the last thing I wanted to do was tell him his mother was currently our prime suspect in Julianna's murder.

"Where's Levi?" I asked Ellie when I arrived at the Hut.

"We had a fight and he left."

"Oh, honey, I'm so sorry. Do you want to talk about it?"

Ellie shrugged.

"Let's grab a table outside." I looked at Ellie's waitress, who was sitting at the counter reading a magazine. She nodded that it was fine if Ellie took a break. Things were slow anyway.

I grabbed a couple of sodas and led Ellie outside. It was another gorgeous day, and I hoped the infectious nature of being at the beach, where everyone was laughing and playing, would go a long way toward lightening her mood.

"So what happened?" I asked after we settled onto a bench overlooking the lake. It was a warm day, but the bench was protected from the late-afternoon sun.

"I don't know exactly. He showed up a little while ago. He seemed to be in a good mood. He kissed me hello and told me about his hike. He seemed really happy."

"And then?" I prompted.

"He said you were going to stop off to talk to Salinger, so you'd be a little late. I mentioned how hard all this has been on you, and how much easier it would have been if Zak had been here this week. He said something about a man needing to do what he had to do to further his career, and the next thing I knew, we were fighting about his job offer."

Ellie looked at me with tears in her eyes. "I think he's going to take the job."

I felt myself begin to panic. I couldn't imagine my life without Levi, and I *really* couldn't imagine what Ellie was going through.

"Did he say as much?" I asked.

"No. Not specifically. But he didn't say he wasn't going to take it either. I really thought that once he thought about it, he'd realize moving was the last thing he wanted to do, but I can sense that he's seriously considering it. He keeps talking about what a huge opportunity this is. He gave me a ton of examples of college coaches who eventually got jobs for pro teams. There's a sparkle in his eye now that I haven't seen for a while."

"He did have a tough go of it at the high school this past winter," I admitted.

"The toughest. And he's facing a tough year in the fall if he can't find a good assistant. I understand why he'd be looking for a way out."

"I'm sure Levi realizes the challenges he's facing are only temporary. I doubt he'll make a life-changing decision based on a temporary setback. Still, I can see how he could be seduced by the glamor of a college-level job."

"What are we going to do?" A single tear slid down Ellie's cheek.

I placed my hand over hers. "I don't know. I don't think we can stand in his way if that's what he really wants." I looked at Ellie. "I guess you could go with him."

"He hasn't exactly asked me to go, and it's not like we're married or even engaged."

"I'm sure if he takes the job he'll ask you to go. He probably figures asking you to give up your life here is premature if he hasn't even decided to take the job yet."

"Maybe. Or it could be that Levi is doing what he always does. The minute things get serious he panics and runs. He's done it in every other relationship he's had. I don't know why I thought ours would be any different."

I didn't say anything; Ellie wasn't wrong and we both knew it. Levi's pattern was to run the minute things got too real. He'd been doing it his entire life. I just never imagined he'd run from Ellie, or that he'd run so far away.

Chapter 9

Thursday, July 16

I'd noticed Kelly still wasn't back to work when I'd dropped by the Beach Hut to talk to Ellie the day before. Kelly and her seemingly violent boyfriend were very much on my mind in spite of everything else that was going on. I decided to stop by to try once again to speak to her. I doubted she'd confide in me, but I figured I had nothing to lose by trying.

I parked my truck on the street. I'd left Charlie with Jeremy because I planned to drop in on Salinger as well while I was in town. I crossed the street, walked down the sidewalk, and knocked on the door. Surprisingly, Kelly opened the door after the first knock. She looked both shocked and dismayed when she saw me standing on her stoop.

"Zoe. I thought you were the UPS guy. I'm expecting a delivery."

Kelly had on a long-sleeved shirt and a pair of faded jeans. She wore a ton of makeup, but I could still make out a nasty bruise under her eye.

"I was in town to talk to Salinger and figured I'd stop by to see how you were feeling."

"Salinger?" A look of panic crossed Kelly's face.

"About the dead woman in my pool," I explained.

Kelly let out a long breath. "I heard about that. I thought it was an accident."

"There may be more going on than we initially believed."

"Wow. If that poor woman was murdered I hope you figure out who did it."

"Yeah, me too."

"Was there something specific you needed?" Kelly asked. I could see she wasn't going to invite me inside. I glanced behind her. She appeared to be alone.

"Nothing specific," I answered. "Ellie has been worried about you, so I told her I'd stop by to see if you were feeling better."

Kelly smiled, but the emotion didn't reach her eyes. "I'm doing better. I should be back to work by the weekend. I want to be sure I'm completely well. This flu has been pretty nasty, and I don't want to infect anyone."

The UPS truck pulled up while Kelly was speaking. The man came to the door, asked her to sign his delivery order, and then handed her a medium-sized box. I noticed the flash of pain across her face as she accepted it.

"Here, let me help." I grabbed the box from her arms and walked inside. "You've been sick. I'm sure you don't have your strength back."

"Thanks. You can just leave it on the table." Kelly nodded toward the dining table.

I set the box down and noticed a hole in the kitchen wall. Kelly saw me looking at it.

"Mouse in the wall," Kelly explained. "I guess I got a little overzealous trying to catch the little bugger."

"I can bring over some supplies and repair it," I offered.

"You know how to fix a wall?"

"My dad made sure I knew how to take care of basic home repairs," I explained.

"Thanks, but I'm sure Jason will fix it when he gets home from work."

"I haven't seen Jason for a while. How's he doing?"

Kelly averted her eyes. "He's fine. I guess you heard he got fired from that construction job he had, but he's been doing okay taking on odd jobs when he can get them."

"Yes, I did hear the construction gig didn't work out. That's too bad. It helps to have a steady paycheck."

"Yeah, well, he does okay."

Kelly stood in the middle of the room, fidgeting. I could tell she wanted me to leave but wasn't sure how to ask me to do it without seeming rude.

"You know, they have a line of professional makeup at that new boutique in town. I believe it's being marketed as a way to cover signs of aging, but it should work well on bruises too."

Kelly brought her hand to her eye. "You can tell?"

"I can tell. Can I help?"

"No. I'm just a klutz. I really need to be more careful."

I took a deep breath and took a chance. "I know you aren't a klutz. And unless you punched a hole in your kitchen wall with your eye, I'm willing to bet you aren't responsible for either the hole or the bruise. If someone is hitting you—if Jason is hitting you—I can help."

Kelly began to cry. "Please don't tell anyone. I can handle this. Jason has just been really mad since he lost his job, and sometimes he drinks too much. We talked it out after the last time, and he agreed to get counseling. He's been better the past few days. Really."

I placed my hand over Kelly's. "I won't say anything. For now," I clarified. "But if Jason starts drinking again you have to promise me that you'll call me. I'll come and get you any time of the day or night."

"I will. I promise."

"I don't mean to be negative, but very few abusive relationships have happy endings."

"I know. But ours will be different. You'll see."

"I really do hope so. You know, Levi told me that they broke ground on the strip mall they're building just outside of town, if Jason is looking for a job."

Kelly looked interested. "Do you think they're hiring?"

"I don't know for sure, but I don't suppose it would hurt to look into it."

"Okay. Thanks. I'll let Jason know. I'm sure he'll calm down a bit once he gets the job thing figured out."

After I left Kelly's apartment I headed over to Salinger's office. He met me in the lobby himself and walked me back to his office. He poured me a cup of coffee and indicated that I should take a seat.

"You okay? You look spooked."

"I'm fine," I answered. "I was visiting a friend. She's having trouble with her boyfriend. I guess I'm just worried about her. What have you found out?"

"Trouble with a boyfriend? Is this the sort of trouble with a boyfriend I should know about?"

"Not yet, but I'll let you know if it becomes that sort of thing. So about the timeline?"

Salinger took out a sheet of paper and pushed it in front of me. "Here's what I came up with after speaking to everyone again."

I looked at the notes while Salinger narrated.

"After dinner everyone staying at the house went into the living room to have a drink. That was at around seven o'clock."

I looked at the diagram and waited for him to continue.

"Shortly after that, at around seven twenty, Helen Zimmerman and Pierre Bordeau excused themselves to retire to the sitting room upstairs to discuss the wedding. About ten minutes later, Longines Walters announced he had a headache and went upstairs to the room he's sharing with Pierre."

I knew Helen had given Pierre, Longines, Jimmy, and Eric and Cindy bedrooms on the second floor, while Julianna, Darlene, Tasha, and Nikki had been provided with accommodations on the first. Pierre and Longines were sharing a room, as were Julianna and Tasha and Darlene and Nikki.

"According to general opinion, Eric had been coming on to Julianna all evening. At approximately seven fifty, Cindy made a comment that indicated she had lost her tolerance for his behavior and stomped out of the room. Eric followed her upstairs a few minutes later. It was at that point, around eight, that Julianna excused herself and left the room. She announced to the others that she was going out for some fresh air, but no one actually saw her leave the house."

I did a quick mental calculation. At that point only Jimmy, Tasha, Nikki, and Darlene would have been left in the living room. Theoretically, they all provided alibis for one another. If Eric and Cindy were together, and Pierre and Helen were together, that only left Longines alone.

"Jimmy and Tasha left the room next," I remembered.

"Yes. According to pretty much everyone left downstairs, Jimmy and Tasha went up to Jimmy's room at approximately eight ten. Nikki excused herself to go to the powder room a few minutes later, and Darlene confirmed that she went into the kitchen to get a beer. It was then that she saw her aunt Helen come down the stairs, grab a bottle of wine, and head out the back door."

"Did you ask Helen about that?" I wondered.

"I did. She said all the planning had been stressful, so she decided to take a few minutes for herself and head down to the beach. She said she didn't specifically look toward the pool, but she didn't notice anything odd either. She claimed she didn't return to the house until after you found the body."

"I remember her coming into the living room from upstairs after I went into the house to inform everyone what was going on. She must have used the back staircase to return upstairs."

"According to Darlene, after she grabbed the beer she had gone into the kitchen to get, she returned to the living room to find Nikki and Eric talking. I confirmed that Eric came back downstairs at the same time Nikki returned from the powder room. You came home at approximately eight fifty and found the body."

"That sounds right. I called you and then went inside. Darlene, Nikki, and Eric were talking. Mrs. Zimmerman came downstairs a few minutes later. Jimmy and Tasha came down a few minutes after that."

"That tracks with what I remember and what was reported to me," Salinger confirmed. "Neither Pierre nor Longines came down until I asked someone to go upstairs to fetch them."

"So assuming Helen is telling the truth and Julianna wasn't yet in the pool at the time she headed down to the beach, Julianna would have been murdered between eight fifteen and eight fifty."

"Yes," Salinger agreed. "That appears to be the window, based on witness accounts. The ME puts the time of death between eight and eight thirty."

I thought about the sequence of events. The only houseguests who appeared to never have been alone were Jimmy and Tasha. Pierre was alone when Helen left, as was Helen. Cindy was alone when Eric left her, and although Eric had returned to the group, it could have been possible for him to leave the room he shared with Cindy, kill Julianna, and then return to the living room. Nikki was alone during the time she said she was in the bathroom, and Darlene was alone in the kitchen both before and after seeing Helen leave. Longines appeared to have been alone the entire evening.

"What now?" I asked.

"I guess we keep looking." Salinger shrugged.

"I wonder where Julianna went after she left the house at eight if she wasn't killed until between eight fifteen and eight thirty."

"I'm having the ME take another look at the body. Maybe he'll find something that will point us in a direction."

If Helen left the house at eight fifteen and went to the beach, and Julianna wasn't yet in the pool, nor did Helen pass her coming or going from the beach, Julianna must have still been in the house, I realized. Everyone had assumed she'd gone outdoors because that's where she told them she was going, but what if she really took the back stairs through the kitchen and went upstairs when Helen left the house? I tried to remember who was still upstairs at the time Helen left the house. I came up with Pierre, Longines, Cindy, and Jimmy and Tasha. My money was on one of them as the killer.

When I left Salinger's office and returned to my truck I noticed I had a text from my mom, asking me to meet her at the dress shop in town for the final fitting of my dress. My mom had ordered it from one of the European boutiques she was familiar with from her world traveler days, but due to the fact that I was height impaired, we'd had to have the dress hemmed. A lot.

Mom reminded me to bring the shoes I planned to wear, so a quick stop at the house was in order. On my way up the stairs I ran into Cindy, who was on her way out by the look of things.

"Are you going into town?" I asked.

"I'm going home. No offense, but it's ridiculous to be here this far ahead of the wedding. Helen insisted on it, but I've had enough of Eric's flirting. I'm leaving."

"I'm sorry to hear that," I lied politely. "Will you return when the wedding gets closer?"

Cindy looked uncertain. "It depends. I may head to Europe. The ridiculous agreement I have with Eric requires that I remain in this sham of a marriage for three more years, but that doesn't mean I have to spend every minute with the moron."

The moment she'd uttered the words I could tell she regretted them.

"Look at me, going on and on about my problems. I really shouldn't burden you with what will turn out to be no more than a lovers' quarrel," she attempted to cover.

"It's okay," I assured her. "I've been around Eric enough to realize you have cause to be angry. I know I would be. And I don't blame you for leaving. Do you need a ride to the airport?"

"No. I have a car coming."

"Before you go, I was wondering if you could help me out with something."

Cindy looked at her watch. "I have a couple of minutes."

"I just spoke to Sheriff Salinger. He's trying to complete his report on Julianna's death and wondered who was upstairs at the time. I know you and Eric went up shortly after Mrs. Zimmerman, Pierre, and Longines did. Did you see any of them there?"

"No. I could hear Helen and Pierre arguing when I passed the sitting room, though. It sounded like Julianna had convinced him to leave and take on another wedding. Helen wasn't happy about his decision, but if the man hadn't been paid I could understand why he wouldn't want to hang around here any longer."

"Darlene mentioned something similar. I'm kind of surprised Pierre even came to Ashton Falls before he had a signed contract."

"Yes, that does seem odd," Cindy agreed.

"Did you see or hear Longines?" I asked.

"No. His bedroom door was closed and I didn't hear anything. Of course he did say he was heading up because he had a headache, so he could have been sleeping."

"And how long after you went upstairs did Eric join you?" I wondered.

"Just a few minutes. He knows what's at risk. He's going to have a coronary when he finds out I'm gone."

I frowned. "Darlene mentioned something about your prenup. I understand you need to remain in the marriage for three more years, but I don't see why Eric will care if you leave. Not that it's any of my business," I quickly added.

"You do seem to be living up to your reputation as a world-class snoop." Cindy almost sounded impressed. "And you're correct: it is none of your business, though if you're going to join the family I guess I can see the advantage in having an ally. Eric married me not because he loved me but because he needed a wife. He charmed and courted me, made me fall in love with him, and then proposed. I was so happy. I really loved him. On the eve of our wedding Jimmy informed me that Eric didn't really love me. He said he was marrying me because his grandfather's will stipulated that he had to be married for five years to the same woman before he could access the bulk of his inheritance. Don't get me wrong; he gets a monthly allowance that's actually very generous, but he wanted it all."

"Ouch."

"Ouch is right. At first I was going to leave, but Eric cut me a deal. If I married him as planned, and kept up the ruse that we were happy, I'd get a substantial payout when he gained access to the entirety of his inheritance. At the time I foolishly thought that if we were married he would learn to love me. Boy, was I wrong. The first year wasn't bad. Eric at least pretended in public that what we had was real. But lately he hasn't even been trying. If I divorce him, he'll need to start over with another woman and I'll get nothing. I guess that gives us both motivation to stay in the relationship."

"I'm so sorry. I'm sure it must be awful to be trapped that way."

"It isn't fun, but I've learned to play the game."

"But why stay with him?" I asked. "Surely you can remain married without participating in each other's lives."

"We can't. Part of the stipulation in the will states that we must sleep in the same room for a minimum of three hundred nights a year. I guess Eric's grandfather wanted to be sure we couldn't do what you just suggested. I can, however, take a few of the away nights I have left this year now if I want to. I really need a break. I'm afraid I'll kill the guy if I have to stay here and watch him paw everything in a skirt."

"Is there someone who keeps track of all this?" I asked. If you asked me, the stipulation in the will was antiquated and, quite frankly, ridiculous.

"His grandmother. You'll meet her next week. Have fun with that one. She's . . . well, you'll see."

Wonderful.

Chapter 10

The entire time I was driving to the dress shop I was rehearsing the discussion I planned to have with my mom. I know she was almost as wedding crazy as Mother Zimmerman, but I really needed her to be on my side. My mother was normally a reasonable person, and I hoped if I could sit her down and share my feelings, I could get her to support me in my subtle war with Zak's mother.

"Did you bring the shoes?" Mom asked the minute I walked in the door.

"I did, but I was wondering if we could talk before we did this."

Mom looked at the seamstress, who just shrugged.

"Let's go outside and sit on that bench in the shade," Mom suggested.

I followed her out the door to the courtyard that was shared by the six small businesses that surrounded it. It was a warm, sunny day, but the temperature was actually very pleasant in the shade. On the weekends the courtyard could become crowded, with shoppers lingering between stores, but today Mom and I were the only two taking advantage of the secluded patio.

"What's on your mind?" Mom asked after we chose a bench and sat down.

The perfectly logical and detailed speech I'd been rehearsing flew out of my mind. I looked at my mom and began to sob. "Everything is all messed up," I cried. "Zak and I had very specific plans as to what we wanted our wedding day to be like, and now everything we wanted has been thrown out the window and been replaced by this media circus that both of us hates."

Mom sat quietly, but I could see I was getting through to her.

"I suppose that you've been dreaming of what my wedding would be, and I'm sure Mrs. Zimmerman has pictured Zak's wedding, but we're the ones getting married and it feels like our dreams don't count or matter."

"You're right." Mom hugged me. "I'm so sorry. I let my enthusiasm take over and haven't really given a lot of thought to what you might want. I figured once you saw the fairy-tale wedding I had planned you'd fall in love with the idea, but I should have known you aren't the Cinderella type."

I'd thought this was going to be much harder. Maybe I should have shed a few tears months ago.

"No," I admitted. "I never was the type to dream of attending a big ball with my prince. Even as a kid, I never dreamed of a big, fancy wedding."

"So what is it you did dream of?" Mom asked.

I laughed. "Honestly, when I was a kid I wanted to have my wedding at Chuck E. Cheese's."

Mom laughed. "And now?"

"Now I want a simple wedding with family and a few close friends on the beach behind the house. I want to wear the simple cotton dress I picked out, and carry a bouquet of daisies. I want Bella and Alex to be co-flower girls and Charlie and Scooter to be co-ring bearers. I want Levi to be the best man and Ellie the maid of honor. What I don't want is a wedding planner, a photo shoot, a fancy dress, or a mixed bouquet."

"Okay," Mom said.

"Okay? Really?"

"Really. It's too late to send the dress I bought back, but maybe I'll save it for Harper. I'll cancel the flowers I ordered and we can order the daisies you want."

"What about Mrs. Zimmerman, Pierre, and *Modern Day Celebrities*?"

Mom used a finger to wipe a tear from my cheek. "Leave them to me."

I hugged my mom. We hadn't been close until she'd moved back to Ashton Falls after she found out she was pregnant with my baby sister Harper, but in the year and a half she'd been in my life we'd become very close. I'd actually been surprised she'd gone as wedding crazy as she had, but looking back on the way I'd handled her wedding last year, I could see that crazy ran in the family.

"I'm so glad you and your mom worked things out," Ellie said a couple of hours later, as we shared a soda during the midafternoon lull at the Beach Hut. "I just hope things go as smoothly with Zak's mom."

"My mom said she'd handle it and I'm going to let her. I've been intentionally avoiding the house all afternoon."

"You and Charlie are welcome to come over to the boathouse this evening. We can order a pizza."

"That sounds nice, but I think I'll go to book club. I wasn't going to, but I'm sure that between the wedding and the honeymoon, wherever we end up going, I'm going to miss next month. You can come along if you want."

"Actually, if you're going to be occupied, I might try to sit down and talk to Levi again. Maybe we can avoid a fight and really communicate about this huge decision he's facing."

"I think that might be a good idea."

"Don't look now," Ellie whispered, "but here comes Tucker Willis."

Tucker is a precocious eleven year old who used to be best friends with Scooter until he moved. He was a nice enough kid, but like Scooter prior to Zak taking him under his wing, Tucker had very little adult supervision and tended to get himself into more than his share of trouble.

"Afternoon, Miss Zoe," Tucker greeted me.

I smiled at the filthy boy with long, stringy hair that looked like it hadn't been washed since Easter.

"What can I do for you, Tucker?"

"You know that old tomcat that's been bothering Mrs. Porterman's chickens?"

"The big white cat with one missing ear?"

"That'd be the one. I finally caught him. I took him over to the Zoo, but Jeremy said I'd need to see you about getting my ten bucks."

Tucker and I had entered into a compensatory relationship two summers back, when he found a cat that had been lost. The owners were offering a reward, and once Tucker realized there was money to be made finding lost pets, he'd become Ashton Fall's number-one pet detective. Tucker had a way with animals and had been successful in finding and trapping strays Jeremy and I hadn't been able to track down. When he began bringing strays to me I'd agreed to pay him, but only after I verified that the stray was actually a stray, and not someone's beloved pet.

"I didn't think we were ever going to trap that cat. I've been trying for two months."

I reached into my pocket and pulled out a handful of bills and loose change.

"Took a while," Tucker admitted. "That old cat is smart. Real smart. Almost seemed a shame to trap him."

"I'm sure Mrs. Porterman will be very grateful that her chickens will no longer be harassed." I handed Tucker two five-dollar bills.

"I heard Scooter is coming to visit."

"He should be here this weekend," I informed the ragged child.

"Last time he was here he said that next time I could come over and swim in your pool."

"I'm sure Scooter would love to have you stop by." I made a mental note to stock up on chlorine. At least a swim would clean Tucker up a bit. "Do you have a phone?"

"No. No phone."

"Why don't you come by on Saturday at around lunchtime? You can plan to eat with us and then maybe take a swim."

Tucker grinned from ear to ear.

"Would you like an ice cream cone before you go?" Ellie asked. "On the house."

"Chocolate?"

"Chocolate. Go on inside and tell the waitress I said it was okay to give you an extra big scoop."

"Thanks." Tucker headed indoors.

"Cute kid," Ellie commented.

"In spite of the fact that he's filthy most of the time he really is a great kid," I agreed.

"Don't you think you should have called Jeremy to confirm Tucker really did bring in that nuisance cat?"

I shrugged. "He hasn't lied to me in the past. I have no reason to think he'd start now."

I began to scoop up my loose change to transfer it back into my pocket. Ellie handed me the button I'd found the other day. It seems I'd never taken it out of my pocket.

"That looks like one of the buttons from the blouse Julianna had on the day she was here," Ellie said. "I remember it because the shape is so unique."

"I found it on the floor of Zak's office."

Ellie looked at me. "Do you think Julianna was snooping around in Zak's office before she died?"

I considered Ellie's question. "Maybe. Someone has been nosing around in there. Actually, I'm fairly convinced that more than one someone has been snooping in there. I just can't seem to catch them in the act. Still, if Julianna was in Zak's office, I wonder if that had anything to do with her death."

"Maybe you should mention the button to Salinger," Ellie suggested.

"Yeah. I think I will."

"How are things going with the investigation? There's nothing like a good mystery to get your mind off things."

I shared my conversations with Salinger and Cindy.

"Wow. That's brutal. I can't imagine what I'd do if I was all set to marry someone I truly loved only to find out he was using me to get at his inheritance."

"I know. The whole thing is so odd. I can't imagine why his grandfather wrote his will the way he did. I mean, I know people used to write marriage contingencies into wills, but things have changed. Marriage isn't looked at the same way it used to be."

"I imagine it's about control," Ellie speculated. "Some people need to control the ones they love even from the grave."

"Creepy. I look at Helen, who's a total control freak, and now I have to consider this other relative, and I have to wonder if I'm marrying into a family of crazy people."

Ellie laughed. "Maybe, but Zak is great. I think he managed to avoid the crazy gene. Is he still going to be back in the morning?"

"Yeah." I smiled. "I spoke to him briefly this morning. He's picking up the kids today and they'll be flying overnight. He should land in Bryton Lake around eight tomorrow morning. I can't wait to see him. It feels like he's been gone a year."

"It has been a hectic week. I'm sure it does feel like a year."

I looked out over the calm, peaceful lake. I hadn't been exaggerating when I'd said it felt like a year. If I knew a month ago what I knew now, I would have suggested that Zak and I sneak away for a quiet wedding and *then* tell everyone we were married.

"I just hope my mom is successful with Mrs. Zimmerman and the wedding crew so that Zak won't have to deal with it when he gets home. I'm sure he's going to be exhausted."

"I'm sure once the wedding planner finds out Zak has no intention of signing a contract he'll be out the door," Ellie pointed out.

"I hope so. Maybe I can get rid of Nikki before she takes any embarrassing photos."

"Yeah, about that . . ."

"What?" I demanded.

"I think we were right that Julianna was giving photos to Bridget."

Ellie pulled up a photo on her phone and handed it to me.

"Oh, God."

The photo was of me in my bra and underwear with a green moisturizing mask on my face. My frizzy hair was sloppily pulled into a topknot and I had a toothbrush in my mouth. The caption under the photo said, "America's fourth most-eligible bachelor has landed himself a Frankenbride."

"How did Julianna even get this picture?" I groaned.

"Do you remember when it might have been taken?" Ellie asked.

"Yeah. It must have been after I got home on Monday. I was in my own bathroom, getting ready for bed. My bedroom door was locked from the inside."

"There must be a camera hidden in your room."

I silently prayed that the ground would open up and swallow me. What kind of a warped degenerate would hide a camera in someone's bathroom? I could only imagine what even more embarrassing photos could be lurking about.

"What am I going to do?" I asked.

"I don't know," Ellie admitted. "I don't have a lot of experience with celebrity stalking, but I doubt a magazine would publish anything truly obscene."

"Where did you get this?" I demanded.

"From Hazel."

"Hazel has seen it? Where did she get it?"

"I'm afraid she got it from your grandfather, who received it in an e-mail from Nick. I imagine it's been making the rounds."

"That decides it. I'm going to have to move."

Ellie laughed. "It really isn't that bad. Yes, a lot of your body shows, but no more than when you wear a bikini, and *everyone* has seen you in a bikini. And yes, it is unfortunate that you happened to decide to moisturize on that particular night, but you don't look any worse than you did last Halloween, when you dressed as the Bride of Frankenstein. I mean really," Ellie looked at the photo, "you actually look kind of adorable."

I started laughing. I was pretty sure I was having a nervous breakdown, but all of a sudden I found myself agreeing with Ellie. I did look adorable. Of course I was still going to kill Bridget once Zak's attorney tracked her down. Which reminded me that I needed to call Zak's attorney before any more *adorable* photos showed up online.

Luckily, by the time I arrived at book club everyone had seen and reacted to the photo and I'd had time to gain some perspective and calm down even more. When I learned from my dad that my mom had seen the photo I realized my green face on her computer screen was probably the catalyst that caused her to change her mind about the wedding. Looking back, it certainly wasn't my unpolished speech, which I never had gotten around to delivering anyway. Maybe I actually owed Julianna and Bridget a debt of gratitude.

My dad had gone over the house to make certain there were no cameras left behind. I would have done it myself, but I really wanted to avoid Mother Zimmerman until after Zak got home. I had no idea what her reaction was going to be to my mom's decision to let us have the wedding we wanted.

"Maybe you should have a theme wedding." Nick Benson laughed. "Mr. and Mrs. Frankenstein."

"Bite me."

Nick was one of the more outgoing of the seniors who belonged to the book club, and one of my grandpa's best friends. I loved him and knew his teasing was all in fun, but I'd had enough *fun* in the past week to last me a lifetime. On the other hand, it looked like the nightmare I'd been experiencing was almost behind me, so maybe I just needed to lighten up and enjoy the rest of the ride.

"I'm sorry to be teasing you, darling. I'm sure this whole thing is upsetting for you."

"It was. For about two minutes. And then Ellie helped me realize that I've taken a lot more embarrassing pictures on purpose. Granted, most of my photos don't end up all over the Internet, but I've decided to laugh it off and move on with my life. My dad made sure there were no more cameras in the house, and Zak's attorney assured me that the magazine Bridget works for will destroy any remaining photos in their possession. Of course I may decide to use the guest bathroom for a while, just in case."

"I guess that really was kind of creepy."

"Very creepy. I can't help but wonder what Bridget had on Julianna that would cause her to do something like that. Julianna had a good job. Based on what others have told me, it sounds to me like she'd worked hard to get and keep it. I'm sure she must have realized that Pierre was going to be furious if he figured out she was the one who leaked the Frankenbride shot."

"Are you sure Julianna gave Bridget the photos because of some sort of debt?"

"That's what Ellie overheard. Although she didn't exactly hear the entire conversation, so there might have been more going on than we know."

"We may never know for certain," Nick concluded. "I'm going to get some more cake. Do you want some?"

"No, thanks."

The seniors had gotten together to throw me their own bridal shower, complete with punch and cake and even presents. I was touched. This kind of genuine show of affection I could deal with. Whatever Mother Zimmerman had planned for the following night was sure to pale by comparison. Of course Zak would be home by then. Maybe he could put a stop to the whole thing.

I really did miss him. And the kids. I hadn't seen Alex since Christmas, though Scooter had come for a short visit during spring break. I wondered if I would feel as much affection for my own kids as I did for these two special people. To be honest, prior to meeting Alex I'd been pretty sure I didn't even want to have children of my own.

"I didn't expect to see you grinning like the cat who got the milk." Pappy walked up beside me and hugged my shoulder with one arm. "I take it you've recovered from your fifteen minutes of fame."

"I am totally over it."

"You seem downright happy."

"I am. Zak is on his way home with Scooter and Alex. Mom has promised that I can have the wedding Zak and I want. If it weren't for the fact that I still haven't figured out who killed Julianna, things would be perfect."

"Who do you think killed her?" Pappy asked. "Your instincts have always been pretty good."

I thought about it. Pappy was right. I did have good instincts.

"There were nine people in the house at the time Julianna died," I began. "I figure that one of those nine people must have done it. Starting from the top, I can honestly say Mrs. Zimmerman had both motive and opportunity."

"You're saying Zak's mom had motive to kill the assistant to the wedding planner?"

"Based on what I've heard from others. Two different people told me Julianna had convinced Pierre to dump my wedding in favor of some basketball player's."

"Guess that would have got you off the hook."

"Trust me, I would have been thrilled if Pierre and company packed up and moved on, but Mrs. Zimmerman seems really invested in having a celebrity affair."

"So I guess that does give her a motive. What about opportunity?" Pappy asked.

"According to Cousin Darlene, Mrs. Zimmerman left the house during the time Julianna was supposedly outside for air. Cindy, who's married to Cousin Eric, told me that she heard Mrs. Zimmerman and Pierre, the wedding planner, arguing about the other wedding Julianna was pushing for. Still, as much as the woman is driving me to an early grave, I can't believe she would do something quite so desperate."

"Who's desperate?" Hazel asked as she joined us from across the room.

"Zoe's telling me who she thinks might have killed the wedding planner's assistant," Pappy explained.

"Oh, well, don't let me interrupt. Please continue."

I took a breath and gathered my thoughts while most of the other book club members gathered around to listen as well.

"And then there was the wedding planner, Pierre," I continued. "He also had opportunity and motive. He was upstairs alone after Mrs. Zimmerman went out and could easily have gone out to the pool area via the back stairs. As for motive, I imagine he would have been pretty mad if he'd found out that his assistant was leaking photos to a competitor of *Modern Day Celebrities*. It appeared he was somehow in bed with the rag, although I haven't figured out exactly how."

"Anyone else?" Pappy asked.

"Longines Walters. He came along as Pierre's other assistant and was supposed to handle my hair and makeup. I don't know what his motive could have been, but I do know that no one saw him after he went upstairs after claiming to have a headache. He had plenty of opportunity to sneak down the back staircase, push Julianna in the pool, and then go back upstairs. There's also the fact that this is his first time working with Pierre. That may just be a coincidence, but the guy gives me the heebie-jeebies. If I turns out to be him, I won't be surprised."

"Is that the guy you said looks like Fat Elvis?" Hazel asked.

"Yup, that'd be him."

I took a sip of the punch someone had handed me before continuing. I felt a little like Jessica Fletcher, laying out the clues while everyone listened. It was actually pretty awesome.

"And then there's the intern, Tasha Golding. As far as I can tell, neither Cousin Jimmy nor Tasha were alone that night, which, unless they're in on it together, puts them in the clear. I'm still concerned about the fact that Tasha had been working for Pierre free for months, waiting for a paid position, which Julianna's death provides, *and* I found Jimmy going through Zak's things on the first day he arrived. Still, I don't see how going through Zak's stuff would relate to Julianna's death."

"Okay, so that's five of the nine. Who else is on your list?" Nick asked.

"Cousin Eric and his wife, Cindy, fought and went upstairs. Eric returned to the living room later, while Cindy stayed behind on the second floor. That gave them opportunity because they were both alone at one point. Eric came on to Julianna, which on the surface gives Cindy motive, but Julianna rejected him, which on the surface gives him motive, but after speaking with Cindy, I can see there's no love lost between them, so I've moved them to the bottom of the list."

"That's seven of the nine," Nick continued to count down.

"Darlene is the youngest cousin," I continued. "She's only seventeen and seems more interested in partying than anything else. Technically, she was alone when Nikki went to the bathroom, but I don't see her as the guilty party. For one thing, she doesn't appear to have a motive.

"Which bring us to Nikki Nicholson, who works for *Modern Day Celebrities*. She was alone for a short time while she supposedly went to the bathroom. She could have told Darlene she was going there but gone out onto the patio instead. The timing of her bathroom break seems to line up pretty closely with Julianna's time of death, but it also matches the time Darlene was in the kitchen to get a drink, so it seems Darlene would have seen her if she left by the back door."

"Unless she went out the front door," Hazel offered. "Based on what you said, the living room was empty at that time. Nikki could have gone out the front door and then walked around the house."

"True," I had to agree.

"Did she have motive?" Pappy asked.

"If Nikki found out Julianna was sneaking photos to a competitor that would give her motive. Logically, she should be at the top of the list, but I just don't know."

"And why is that?" Pappy asked.

"She seems really nice. Still, if I had to prioritize the suspects based on a point system, taking into account both motive *and* opportunity, I guess I would have to say that Pierre, Nikki, and Mrs. Zimmerman have the highest scores. All three of them had relatively strong motives and reasonable opportunities. That trio would be followed by Eric and Cindy. They had opportunity but weak motives, as does Longines. Jimmy was nosing around in Zak's office and Tasha most likely gained a paid position because of Julianna's death, but neither of them appear to ever have been alone. Which leaves us with Darlene bringing up the rear."

"So what's your next move?" Nick asked.

"I have no idea. If Mom does what she promised, half of these people will be gone by the end of the day tomorrow. We may never know who pushed Julianna into the pool."

Chapter 11

Friday, July 17

In my dream I was falling. There was nothing surrounding me as I fell into the dark abyss. I saw the moments of my life play across my mind as I struggled to find a foothold in the surfaceless chamber. As I fell, memories from my past merged with the promise of my future. I found that I was no longer afraid. I closed my eyes and relaxed into the fall, unaware of where it would lead but free from the need to know. I felt the burden I'd been carrying lighten as I embraced the uncertainty.

In the corner of my mind I could hear a rustling. It didn't seem to be congruent with my dream. I tried to ignore it, but when Charlie started to growl, I felt myself pulled from the realm of my subconscious into one of texture and form. I slowly opened my eyes and looked around the dark bedroom. A glance at my clock showed me that it was only 2:20.

I leaned up onto an elbow and tried to figure out what had awakened me. And then I realized. The rustling was coming from the baby monitor I'd left on the nightstand next to the bed.

I pulled on a pair of sweatpants I had discarded next to the bed, grabbed the key to the office, told Charlie to stay, and then headed down the hall. In the last instant, just as I opened the door and forced my way inside, it occurred to me that perhaps I should have brought a weapon.

"What are you doing in here?" I asked.

A man who was not a man but looked an awful lot like Longines, if he was thin and female, turned and stared at me. "Oh, good. I was about to come to fetch you. I found the hidden safe, but for the life of me I can't get it open. I don't suppose you have the combination?"

My mouth hung open as I considered the request of the person in front of me. "You aren't a man."

The woman looked down at her unbound chest. "No. I guess I'm not."

"And you aren't fat." I was trying to reconcile the fact that I was looking at Longines's face but someone else's body.

"I suppose now that I have removed my body padding that is obvious. You know, I really should have rethought my disguise. Binding my chest and adding all that padding every day has become most tiresome. To be honest, I didn't think finding the hard drive was going to be this difficult."

"Hard drive?" I asked.

"The one your fiancé copied from that busybody Christianson's computer."

"You're Claudia Lotherman," I accused.

"Yes. I thought you'd already figured that out. Now where is the hard drive?"

I took a deep breath and stood as tall as my five-foot, no-inch frame would allow. "I don't know, and even if I did I wouldn't tell you."

"Oh, really." Claudia smiled a sick sort of grin. I noticed for the first time that she had a gun. "There are eight other people in this house and I will kill them one at a time until you tell me what I want to know."

I knew in my heart that she'd do as she threatened. She'd killed before, she'd almost killed me in Alaska, and I was pretty sure she'd killed Julianna.

"Why did you kill Julianna?" I asked.

Claudia looked bored by my question, but she answered anyway, which told me that she planned to kill me no matter how this little game played out.

"She came upstairs and found me looking through the office. I'm pretty sure she was up here snooping around herself, but the fact that she was as guilty as I didn't seem to matter to her. She threatened to tell you that I was in the office, so I escorted her downstairs and did what I had to do. Now, about the hard drive?"

I looked around the office for a way out. I could try to escape, but she did have a gun and she wasn't afraid to use it.

"I really don't know what Zak did with the hard drive," I answered. "When we got home from Alaska he stashed it somewhere, and I haven't seen it since."

"Can you open the safe?"

"No." I was being completely honest. "Zak has never shared the combination."

I could see Claudia believed me, but I could also tell she wasn't at all happy about the current circumstances. She appeared to be considering the situation.

After a moment she shrugged. "I guess we will have to do this the hard way. Where is your cell phone?" she asked.

"In the bedroom."

"We are going to go and get it. You are going to walk very quietly across the hall. If anyone wakes up and comes to investigate I will kill them. Do you understand?"

"Yes. I understand."

Claudia motioned that I should precede her out the door. We crossed the hall, and I paused at the door. "Charlie is inside. If he sees you, he'll bark. I should go in alone if you don't want anyone else disturbed."

Claudia looked at me. "All right, but if you try anything, your annoying little dog will be the first one to die."

"I'll get the phone and then come right back out. I promise."

I pulled a sweatshirt over my T-shirt, then grabbed my phone and a pair of tennis shoes. I'm not sure why, but I had the feeling I would need them. I hugged Charlie and tiptoed out of the room. I didn't want any more bloodshed. When I returned to the hallway Claudia took my phone and found Zak's number. She dialed him and waited.

When she got an answer she said, "I have your fiancée. If you want to see her alive you will bring me Carter Christianson's hard drive. Call this number when you get to Ashton Falls." Then she hung up.

"What did he say?" I asked.

"He didn't answer, so I left a message. I'm sure we will be hearing from him shortly."

"He's on his way home. I'm sure he's in the air, which is why he didn't answer. He's due to land in Bryton Lake at eight o'clock."

"Very well. Why don't we find a comfy place to wait?"

If Claudia's idea of comfy was a deserted cabin at the edge of town I hated to see what she considered roughing it. As soon as we arrived, she tied me to a chair and then stretched out and fell promptly asleep. Sitting alone in the dark, waiting for the sun to rise and Zak to either come and save me or to end up dead in the attempt, was the longest few hours of my life.

Claudia appeared to have slept soundly until she was awakened by the ringing of my phone. She sat up, picked up the phone, and looked at the caller ID.

She smiled.

"Bring the hard drive you copied from Christianson to the clearing at the end of the logging road at the south end of town. Come alone. If I even think I smell a cop your girlfriend is dead." She hung up without waiting for a reply.

"We're north of town," I informed her.

"I know. You didn't think I was going to bring him to the place I have you stashed, did you? It would be too easy for him to lead others to your location. I am afraid you are going to be a bit less comfortable while you wait for us to return."

"Us?"

"I can't let either of you go until I see if the file has been accessed."

"File?"

Claudia sighed. She looked at me as if I were a tiresome child. "Christianson had a file on his hard drive. It was encoded. When I retrieved the original hard drive from the CIA I realized it had not as yet been accessed, so I thought I was in the clear. After a bit of persuasion, the man I killed in order to obtain the drive told me the person who gave him the hard drive in the first place had made a copy. If I find that the file has been accessed by your nosy boyfriend you are both dead. If the file has not been accessed I'll leave you with at least a chance of getting out of this in one piece."

"What's in the file?" I couldn't help but ask.

"If I tell you, I *will* have to kill you."

"Oh, then never mind."

"I'm going to untie your feet so we can take a little walk. If you try to run I will shoot you."

"Where are we going?" I asked.

Claudia just looked at me.

"I know; if you tell me you'll have to kill me." I sat still while she untied the rope binding my legs to the chair.

"There's one thing I really do want to know. How did you manage to get a job with the wedding planner on such short notice? Is he in on this?"

"He is too stupid to be in on anything. I have been looking for a way to get into your house ever since I found out about the copy of the hard drive. I heard you and cutie pie were getting married, so I arranged to bump into Mrs. Zimmerman at a charity event I knew she would be attending. We got to talking about the wedding, and I convinced her that she would need help. I suggested Pierre, who I knew had a last-minute opening because I had orchestrated it. Once she arranged for Pierre to help with the wedding I created a job for myself."

"You caused the accident the regular stylist was involved in?"

"He's fine, and it was a necessity."

"Still, how did you get Pierre to hire you?"

"I can be very persuasive. Now get walking, and remember, I have a gun at your back."

Claudia walked me across the property and locked me in an underground room that I assumed was some sort of root cellar, although it appeared to be large and deep and I couldn't see the back of it. While I wasn't certain of its size, I was certain it was filled with all sorts of nasty, crawly things. My hands and feet were bound and the space around me was totally dark, although I could feel fresh air coming in from somewhere. At least I wouldn't suffocate. I tried not to panic as I felt something crawl up my arm. It felt like the walls were closing in around me.

I closed my eyes and tried to focus on what I needed to do to get out of there. I assumed Claudia was heading over to the clearing where she'd told Zak to meet her. If he did as she asked and showed up alone, the entire trip shouldn't take more than thirty minutes. I tried to loosen the rope around my hands, but it was secured tightly. If I could see what I was doing maybe I could find something to cut the ropes. The problem was that I couldn't see a thing and was afraid to move lest I make things worse for myself.

Claudia had said she'd let us go if Zak hadn't accessed her file, but I sort of doubted it. She didn't seem the type to leave excess baggage behind. Of course in spite of the fact that she'd kidnapped me twice, I still had no idea what she actually looked like. Her superpower was the invisibility that was brought about by the myriad disguises she seemed to forever be changing in and out of.

In her Longines costume she in no way resembled the eighty-year-old woman who had called herself Ethel Montros in Alaska. She also didn't resemble any of the women I'd seen photos of after Zak's discovery of her identity. Maybe she would let us live. It wasn't like we would be able to pick her out of a lineup.

I realized that cowering in the dark wasn't going to get me anywhere. I needed a plan. I needed a good one, and I needed it fast. The problem was that my mind was totally paralyzed with fear. Fear that Claudia would kill Zak and that I'd never see Charlie again. Fear that I would miss my own wedding and that I wouldn't grow old with Zak, Levi, and Ellie. I thought of my parents and my baby sister Harper. I really wanted to be around to be the big sister she deserved.

I closed my eyes against the darkness, took a deep breath, and forced myself to think logically. There had to be something I could do.

The cabin Claudia had brought me to was pretty isolated, so I doubted that screaming would help. She had taken my phone, so calling someone for help was likewise out of the question. I thought about a way to escape, but in my current circumstances coming up with one seemed unlikely at best. I supposed I could try to loosen the rope tied around my wrist. I knew that my attempt to free myself would be fruitless, but at least it would give me something to do.

Although I seemed to be waiting for what felt like days, I couldn't think of a single thing to do to save myself. I'd gone over every scenario in my head dozens of times, but there didn't appear to be an answer. I began to get even more worried than I already had been when no one came for me. They should have been finished by now. Maybe Claudia never had planned to bring Zak back here. Maybe she'd gotten what she wanted, killed him, and then disappeared from the mountain, leaving me to die in this dark, dank hole in the ground.

The longer I waited the more terrified I became. At some point I'd have to take a chance and do something. I had no idea what that something was going to be, but I couldn't just sit here until I died without at least trying to save myself. I'd been working the ropes, but I was getting nowhere. Claudia certainly knew how to tie a knot.

I was on the verge of plunging into a full-on panic attack when I heard voices.

"I promised your girlfriend that if you cooperated I'd give you a chance to live. I may be a thief, a spy, even a murderer, but I am an honorable woman."

I heard a scraping sound, as if a lever was being moved. I waited quietly.

A flash of bright light blinded me as Claudia lifted the door to my dark chamber.

I closed my eyes against the pain.

"Get in," I heard Claudia say.

I heard movement, and then the darkness returned as the door was once again closed.

"Zak."

"Oh, God, Zoe, are you okay?"

"Yeah. I'm okay. I can't see you. My hands and feet are tied. I can't move."

"Stay where you are."

I heard a rustling sound as Zak made his way over to where I was sitting. I sensed his body near me. I wanted to reach out, but I couldn't. I felt a hand on my face. Zak pulled me into his arms and hugged me tighter than he ever had. I felt dampness on my cheek, but I was pretty sure the tears were his, not mine.

"I thought I'd lost you," Zak cried. "I was sure she was going to kill us both."

Zak pulled my face toward his and kissed me. A long, desperate kiss that communicated his fear. I wanted to hug Zak back, but my hands were still tied behind my back, so I simply allowed my tears to mix with his.

"I'm okay," I assured him after he ended the kiss. "We both are. At least for now."

Zak squeezed me one last time before allowing a small space between us. "I'm going to untie you. I can't see what I'm doing, but I think I can get you loose."

I sat as still as I could while Zak worked on my feet, which were in front of me.

"Do you have any idea how we're going to get out of here?" I asked.

"Claudia locked the door. I got a good look at the lock while I was waiting for her to unlock it and put me in here. I doubt we'll be able to get out that way."

"Isn't that way the only way?" I asked.

"I don't think so," Zak replied as my feet came free. "Turn around and I'll get your hands."

I did as he instructed. "What do you mean, you don't think so? We're in an underground cellar. It seems to me that the door we came in through is the only way out."

"I don't think we're in a cellar," Zak told me as he worked on the rope around my hands. "I think we're in one of the outlets to the mine system I used to play in as a kid."

Long before we were born, gold had been mined in the hills surrounding the lake from which the town had sprung. Back then, it had been called Devil's Den.

"So there should be another way out," I realized.

"I hope so."

"But we can't see anything. What's to stop us from wandering around these mines forever without finding another outlet?"

"Not a damn thing," Zak answered.

I felt the rope loosen around my hands. Zak worked it free and then rubbed by wrists, which had gone numb due to lack of circulation.

"My dad used to warn me about playing in the mines. He told me stories about cave-ins and drop-offs that plunged several stories."

"Both distinct possibilities," Zak admitted.

"Let's at least try the door," I suggested.

Zak pulled my face to his and kissed me. "That's the plan. We'll try everything we can to get out that way, but if we can't, venturing into the mine may be the only chance we have."

"Maybe someone will find us," I said.

I listened as Zak scooted away from me. "That's very unlikely. This area has been deserted for decades. The road is completely overgrown. Most people don't even know that cabin is here."

"I wonder how Claudia found it. She isn't from this area."

"I don't know. She didn't say and I didn't ask," Zak admitted.

I listened as he pounded on the door. I could tell he was trying to see if there was any give in the structure. There was absolutely no light coming from around the entrance, which led me to believe it was sealed tightly. The walls surrounding us were covered with wood. I could feel the rough texture now that my hands were free. I imagined that the entrance to the cave system had been reinforced with wooden planks, but I was willing to bet that the deeper you traveled into the mine system, the more likely you were to find dirt walls. Maybe we could tunnel out?

Even as I considered this option, I knew that was a lot less realistic than taking a chance on finding another outlet.

I could hear Zak moving around. I guessed he was looking for something to use as a tool.

"It looks like Claudia is going to get away again." I sighed.

"Not necessarily. I installed a tracking program on the copy of the hard drive I gave her. If she doesn't think to look for it, she won't know to compensate for it. I called Salinger and told him what was going on before I headed to the clearing. He's going to try to head her off before she leaves the mountain."

"Maybe he'll find us," I hoped.

"Possible but doubtful. I insisted he not follow me to the clearing. I figured Claudia would be watching. Salinger knows I was headed there, but he doesn't know Claudia brought us here."

I wiped the dirt from my face that had become loose as Zak worked on the door. "Too bad you didn't put a tracking device on your body."

"I did. Claudia found it. I hope she's satisfied that she outsmarted me and won't go looking for the program I uploaded."

"She told me that she'd only let you go if you hadn't decrypted the file she was looking for."

"I guess the fact that I've been too busy with my new software program to give much time to the contents of the hard drive turned out to be a good thing."

A cloud of dirt rained down on us as Zak continued to try to work the door. At this rate, his attempt to open the door was going to cause a cave-in.

"I don't think we're getting out this way," he said.

"I was afraid of that."

Zak crawled over and sat down next to me. He put his arm around me and pulled me close to his body. I could feel his heart beating under my cheek and suddenly I was no longer afraid.

"So do we wait or do we look for a way out?" he asked.

"Does everyone know what happened?" I asked.

"No. Not everyone. I figured Claudia was watching the house. I called Salinger from a pay phone at the airport as soon as I got Claudia's message. Then I dropped the kids off at Ellie's. I explained to them what was going on but instructed them not to tell anyone. I went to our house and snuck up the back stairs, grabbed the hard drive, and snuck back out. No one saw me."

"Poor Charlie is locked in the bedroom."

"Levi was going to go pick him up."

"Salinger, Ellie, and Levi all know we're missing. Maybe we should give them a chance to find us before we head deeper into the mine," I suggested. "Salinger might not know where we are, but I would think he would consider looking for us in deserted cabins. There aren't that many in the area."

"If you want to wait we'll wait." Zak pulled me onto his lap. He leaned back against the wall and I leaned into his chest. In that instant I felt like I could stay that way forever.

"So how was your week?" I asked.

Zak laughed. "It wasn't my best."

"Did you get your computer glitch fixed?"

"I did. Actually, I found the hacker who successfully staying one step ahead of me for almost eight days."

"You had him arrested?" I asked.

"I hired him."

I sat up straight, knowing my look of shock was wasted in the darkness. "What? This guy wastes a week of your life playing some stupid computer game with your client's system and you hire him?"

"We talked about taking on a partner," Zak reminded me. "And this guy is good. Really good. In fact, I'm pretty sure he let me find him. I'm not sure I would have otherwise."

"But he broke into your customer's system," I reminded him. "Isn't that illegal?"

"Yeah, it's illegal. The thing is that the guy didn't do any damage, and he definitely could have. I'm pretty sure he just wanted to get my attention."

"He could have sent you a résumé and applied for a job," I countered. I was beginning to think Zak had completely lost his mind.

"He did, but I didn't take it seriously. I guess he figured I needed a demonstration of what he could do."

I shook my head and closed my eyes. Zak really had lost it. "If this guy has the level of skill you've indicated he must have tons of credentials. Why didn't you take him seriously?"

"Because he's a sixteen-year-old high school student. Or at least he was a high school student. He dropped out after his mom died last winter."

"The guy who has had you jumping through hoops for over a week is sixteen?" I clarified.

"Yup."

"That's—"

"Amazing?" Zak filled in.

"I was going to say crazy. Are you sure he isn't lying about his age?"

"I'm sure. You'll like him. His name is Pi. Or at least that's what he goes by."

"Pie?" I asked.

"Pi as in the number sequence most commonly represented by 3.1415."

"I see. And he's nice?"

"A bit of a smart-ass, but yeah, he's nice."

I closed my eyes and leaned into Zak's body. I wanted to memorize the feel of him next to me. There was a good chance we wouldn't make it out of there, but I was determined that our last minutes would count for something.

"You know I love you," I whispered.

Zak tightened his arms around me. "I do. And you know I love you."

"I do."

"It's been a tough week," Zak admitted. "I'm sorry we fought."

"It was my fault."

"No. It was mine. I should have told my mother right away that we had our own wedding and honeymoon plans. I tried to appease her, but in the process I made you miserable. I promise you, when we get out of here—and we will—I'm going to fix everything. We're going to have the wedding we wanted."

I smiled. I was sure my mom had already done a lot to put things right, but I didn't say as much. I knew Zak needed to take a stand with his mother, the way I had taken a stand with mine. Suddenly, I was looking forward to next week, not dreading it the way I had even a day ago.

"Levi was offered a job as an assistant coach at the state college," I informed Zak. It seemed to help to chat about everyday life while we waited for someone to rescue us—or not.

"Really? Good for him. He's worked hard and deserves it."

"While that may be true, if he takes the job it means he'll be moving away from Ashton Falls."

"The state college isn't all that far away. He can come to visit and we can go visit him there. It won't be the same as having him here every day, but it won't be too bad."

I didn't want to start another argument, but I didn't agree. If Levi moved away it was going to be very bad indeed. I was used to having my best friends in my life every day.

"What about Ellie?" I asked.

"What about Ellie?"

"She's in love with Levi. I doubt she's going to be happy seeing him one weekend a month."

"I guess I just assumed she'd go with him," Zak said.

"As of the last time I spoke to her, Levi hadn't asked her to go. And even if he did, she has a business to run. Her life is here. I don't think she wants to move."

"You'd really miss them," Zak realized.

"Of course I would. We've been best friends since we were in kindergarten. I love Levi and Ellie. I depend on them. I can't imagine my life without them."

Zak tightened his arms around me. "Don't worry. It will all work out."

I wasn't so certain, but I supposed we had more important things to worry about at the moment.

"How long should we wait before we set off looking for another opening?" I asked.

"I don't know. Something occurred to me while we've been sitting here. Claudia had your phone. She took mine as well. I doubt she would take them with her. Maybe she left them in or near the cabin. Salinger might be able to track us down using the GPS in the phones if she didn't think to turn them off."

"So we should wait."

"Yeah. At least for a couple of hours. If the phones are on, Salinger will have realized we never checked in and track us down by then."

I leaned my head against Zak's shoulder. "So what should we do in the meantime?"

It was pitch black, but I swear I could see him grin.

"Besides that."

"It's been over a week."

"Maybe, but I'm not taking off a thing until I can see what keeps crawling up my arm."

Zak laughed. "Fair enough." He tightened his grip around me and kissed me on the top of the head. I felt safe sitting on his lap even though there wasn't a single reason I could think of not to assume we were going to die in this dark, dank hole. I coughed as a cloud of dust filled the chamber.

"What's that noise?" I asked. It was a rumbling sound. Sort of like an earthquake.

Rivers of dirt began to fall on and around us.

"We need to move away from the opening. I think all the digging around I did might have dislodged the structure of the dirt walls."

Zak stood up and pulled me against him. "I'm not positive, but I think there's a very good chance there could be a cave-in right about where we're standing."

"But we have no idea what's ahead of us."

I could feel Zak stretching out his arms to feel the walls around us.

"Here's what we're going to do. I'm taller than you, so I'll go first. If my head hasn't come into contact with anything overhead yours won't either. I'm going to walk slowly with my right hand on the wall to my right and my left hand overhead to feel for a low ceiling. I want you to walk right behind me. Hang on to the waistband of my jeans with your right hand. Whatever you do, don't let go. I want you to reach out your left hand toward the wall. If you feel anything we should be concerned about, let me know."

"Okay." I positioned myself as Zak had instructed.

He walked slowly, one step at a time, feeling the path in front of him with his foot before stepping down. If there was a drop-off hopefully he'd realize it before he fell into it. We moved deeper into the cave until we were well away from the opening.

"We have two choices. We can wait here and hope we've moved far enough away from the potential cave-in or we can keep going."

The idea of continuing into the darkness terrified me, but the thought of being buried alive frightened me even more.

"What do you think?" I asked.

Zak didn't answer right away. I supposed he was considering my question.

"I can feel fresh air coming from the tunnel ahead. There's a good chance there's either an access point or an air vent. In either case, we might be able to get out that way."

"What if there are junctions? I'd hate to get lost."

"That's a legitimate concern, but I'm not sure we have a lot of good choices."

As we paused to consider our choices, a big crashing sound filled the dark chamber. I still couldn't see anything, but I knew that leaving through the doorway we'd originally entered was no longer an option.

"I guess we look for the source of the air," I said as soon as the dust cleared enough for me to speak.

Zak and I forged ahead. One slow and agonizing step at a time. Luckily, our progress thus far had been unimpeded by any real obstacles. It took what seemed like hours, but eventually we came to the place where the fresh air was entering the cave system. It was a small opening a good six feet over our heads

"I'll boost you up," Zak suggested. "If you can climb through you can go for help."

"How far do you think we've come?" I asked.

"Not far. In fact, I'd be willing to bet we're within sight of the cabin."

"And once I get out?" I asked. "The cabin is miles from the road. It will take me hours to walk to the road, catch a ride, and go for help."

"I really don't see another option."

I screamed as another loud crash sounded from behind us.

"The whole thing is going to come down," I cried.

"We could move farther into the cave, but this access is our best shot. Now hang on to my shoulder while I boost you up."

I felt the ground begin to rumble.

"I'm not leaving you here."

Zak put his hands on the sides of my face. At least the light from the opening allowed me to see him. I couldn't help but wonder if this was the last time I would.

"Getting you out of here is our best shot," Zak argued. "Now climb up onto my shoulders."

I kissed Zak and then did as he asked. The only problem was that even with our combined height I couldn't reach the opening, nor did I see anything to grab onto.

"I need to find . . ." Zak began.

"Wait."

Zak stopped talking.

"I think I heard a vehicle pull up," I whispered.

"I can hear it too. It sounds like it's pulling away."

"We're in here," I shouted at the top of my lungs.

"They can't hear us," Zak concluded. "If it was Salinger, he must have seen the cabin was empty and continued on."

"If it was Salinger he won't be back." I realized.

"Probably not."

I felt completely defeated until I heard a barking in the distance.

"Charlie," I screamed.

The barking grew louder. I could hear the car returning.

By now Charlie was barking frantically just outside the opening I was reaching toward.

"What are you doing, you silly dog?" The voice sounded like Levi. "There's nothing out here."

"Levi! If that's you, we're down here."

"Zoe?"

"We're underground," I shouted. "Look for an air vent. It's small."

I waited while Levi located the access point. I could just see his face as he looked down into the hole. "How did you get in there?"

"Long story. You need to find a rope. And fast. The mine is caving in behind us."

"Okay, hang on. I'll see what I can find."

I could hear Levi speaking to someone. Ellie's face appeared in the opening.

"Don't worry. We'll get you out," she assured us. "Levi went for help."

It didn't take long for Levi to get us out once he found a length of rope that had been left in the shed just outside the deserted cabin.

It turned out that Levi and Ellie had decided to look for us while Salinger dealt with Claudia. They'd pulled up in front of the cabin and, as we assumed, quickly saw the cabin was empty and decided to continue on. Charlie, who had been in the backseat of Levi's car, jumped over the seat and out Ellie's open window. Maybe no one could see us, but Charlie knew I was there.

Ellie threw her arms around me and sobbed as Levi pulled me through the small entrance. Charlie ran around me barking until I dropped to the ground and gathered him into my arms. Levi worked to enlarge the opening so Zak could climb the rope and squeeze through.

"Let's go home," Zak said once we were safely in the car.

"What time is it?" I asked.

"Four thirty," Ellie answered.

"Then let's head to the boathouse to hide out until *after* the bridal shower. I'll call my mom and explain what's up. She can make our excuses."

Chapter 12

Several hours later, I was sitting on a lounger at the boathouse staring out at the lake. Scooter and Alex were playing with Bella, Shep, and Karloff on the beach. Zak and Levi were discussing his job offer. Ellie had headed inside the minute that subject came up. I thought about going after her, but I was so tired after my ordeal. The thought of nudging Charlie off my lap and making my way indoors was almost more than I could contemplate.

Still, best friends are supposed to be there for each other. Even when they're physically and emotionally exhausted. It had been a very long and at times terrifying day, but in the end it had turned out okay. Salinger had managed to catch up with Claudia before she left the area, and she was now safely in the hands of federal agents. Zak was not only grateful that the woman had been captured but was doing everything in his power to make sure he made up for the incident, which for some reason he considered to be his fault.

I'd spoken to my mother, and not only had she managed to cancel the bridal shower but she'd made sure that the wedding planner and his crew were gone before the end of the day. Mom had really come through for me in the end. Not only had those guests who weren't relatives left the house but those who were had gone as well. Mom had rented a house for the cousins a good three miles down the beach and, best of all, she'd managed to persuade Mother Zimmerman to stay in the rental until the wedding.

I found I was looking forward to going home to a quiet house with just Zak, Scooter, Alex, and the animals for company. But first I needed to make sure my best friend was okay. I pushed Charlie off my lap and headed inside.

"Long day," I said to Ellie, who was loading the dishwasher.

She paused and looked up at me. "The longest. I don't know what I would have done if we hadn't found you. I can't remember ever being so terrified."

"Yeah, it wasn't fun, but I'm glad Claudia is finally in custody."

"I can't believe she's been staying in your house all week. That's so creepy."

"I knew there was something about Longines I didn't like or trust, but never in my wildest dreams did I think he was Claudia. She really is good at what she does."

"Maybe I should become a master of disguise," Ellie commented.

I frowned. "Why?"

"So I can keep Levi interested."

"Come on, El. Levi is interested and you don't need costumes to keep it that way. I understand why you feel the way you do. And I agree that he's been a bit of a jerk not to include you in his decision more than he has. But he loves you. He loved you before he loved you, if that makes any sense. He's flattered that a big state college wants him and it may have gone to his head just a bit, but in the end I promise he'll sit down and talk this out with you."

"You can't promise that," Ellie pointed out.

"You're right. I can't. But I still think he will. The question is, are you willing to put his happiness over your own if that's what it comes down to in the end?"

Ellie shut the door of the dishwasher and dried her hands on a dishtowel. "What do you mean?"

"If he decides he really does want to take the job, are you willing to go with him?"

Ellie looked out the window. She bit her lip as she contemplated my question. "I don't know. I love Levi, but I think I'd be miserable. I love living in Ashton Falls, where I have friends I've known my whole life. I love running the sandwich shop on the wharf and living in this tiny boathouse. If I gave everything up to follow Levi, he'd have his job but what would I have? I think in the long run I'd resent the fact that I was forced to give up everything."

"I get that." I walked across the room and hugged Ellie.

"What would you do?" Ellie wondered.

What would I do? I loved my life, but I loved Zak more. "If I had to choose between my life in Ashton Falls and Zak, I'd choose Zak."

"Yeah. I figured. Maybe this whole thing should be a wake-up call to me. If I don't love Levi enough to give everything up for him, maybe we shouldn't be together in the first place."

"Don't do anything rash," I cautioned. "Give Levi time. Give yourself time. Maybe it will all work out."

Later that night, I lay in Zak's arms. The kids were asleep, everyone else was gone, and once again equilibrium had been restored in the Zimmerman household. For the first time since Mother Zimmerman had arrived I was actually looking forward to the week ahead. Ellie had promised me a small, low-key bachelorette party, my mom had promised me a smallish, low-key wedding, and Zak had promised me a lifetime of wedded bliss.

"I've been thinking," Zak said softly as he caressed my hair. "Maybe we should write our own vows."

"What?" I sat up straight "You want us to write vows?" I said with panic in my voice. "Vows we say in front of people?"

"I take it you aren't a fan of the idea."

"I love you. You know I do. It's just that I've really been rehearsing the big *I do*. I'd hate to miss out on that."

"We can still say the *I do* part," Zak assured me.

"Yeah, I know. It's just that . . . you're comfortable speaking in front of large audiences. You do it all the time as part of your job. I'm more of a small-audience sort of girl. Or even better yet, a no-audience public speaker. I want to be relaxed on my wedding day, not stressed about remembering what I meant to say but will surely forget. Besides, I have no idea what I would say."

"Just speak from your heart. It doesn't have to be difficult. Here, let's practice."

Zak turned so that we were sitting face-to-face. He took me hands and looked me directly in the eye. "I, Zachary Zion Zimmerman, do take you, Zoe Harlow Donovan, to be my lawfully wedded wife."

I laughed. It seemed ridiculous to be sitting naked in bed practicing our wedding vows.

"I have loved you from the moment I looked into your eyes in the seventh grade and saw your complete disgust and annoyance at my very existence on this earth. I vowed in that moment that one day you would be my wife. It's been a rocky ride, and there have been moments when I've doubted my ability to win your heart, but after thirteen years of waiting, I now stand before my family and friends to share with them the realization of my deepest wish and greatest desire."

Zak's demeanor changed from playful to serious as he continued.

"I, Zak Zimmerman, promise to adopt every stray you bring home, human or animal, regardless of how many we already have. I promise to support all of your crazy schemes and rescue you when those crazy schemes land you in trouble. I promise to always put you first and to be on your side even when you're wrong. I promise to always live up to the faith in me that I see in your eyes and to strive to be the man you deserve. I promise to protect your huge heart from sorrow and pain and to give all of me to you, holding nothing back. But most of all, I promise to love you every day of my life."

"Oh, Zak."

"Your turn." He smiled.

I took a deep breath to get my emotions under control so I could speak.

"Do you need me to get you started?" Zak asked.

I nodded.

"'I, Zoe Harlow Donovan, take you, Zachary Zion Zimmerman, to be my lawfully wedded husband,'" Zak began.

I ignored the tears streaming down my face and the emotion choking my voice and took over.

"When you returned to Ashton Falls with the intention of winning my heart and making a life with me, I was such a mess," I began. "I was filled with so much jealousy and insecurity that I wasn't capable of loving anyone the way you deserved to be loved. Over the past year and a half you have taught me that love can be dependable. It can be counted on to stay strong and see you through, even when the circumstances would dictate otherwise. You ignored my flaws and saw the best in me, and in doing so you made me want to be the woman you believe I am. You loved me when I was insecure, you loved me when I was petty, you loved me when I was crazy, and now I'm crazy in love with you."

I put my hand on Zak's cheek and looked him in the eye. "I promise to limit my meltdowns to one a month and to always put you first. I promise to fill your house with children and your life with spontaneity, but most of all, I promise to love you every day of my life."

Zak kissed me and I melted into his arms. He pulled back a breath. "Now that we've practiced the wedding," he said against my lips, "perhaps we should practice the honeymoon."

"Right there with you."

Soul Surrender publishes May 15, 2015

Soul Surrender picks up the day after *Matrimony Meltdown* ends. Now that Zak and Zoe have their house, their lives, and their wedding back, things seem to be on track once again, until a man is found dead and Zoe is once again pulled into a murder investigation. Zak and Zoe work together to find the killer while Zoe deals with the fact that Levi and Ellie seem to be imploding before her very eyes. Meanwhile Alex shares a shocking piece of news that causes Zak and Zoe to consider taking a huge step that could forever alter their future.

Heavenly Honeymoon publishes June 15, 2015

Recipes for Matrimony Meltdown

Recipes from Kathi:

Cherry Nut Muffins
Mexi-beef Lasagna
Strawberry Éclair Cake
Lemon Cheesecake

Recipes from Readers:

Date and Nut Bars—submitted by Bobby Tobey
Picnic Summer Slaw—submitted by Joanne Kocourek
The Ultimate Baked Beans—submitted by Janel Flynn
Baked Chicken—submitted by Sandra Kerr
Grilled Apricot Pie—submitted by Vivian Shane
Kindergarten Cookies—submitted by Melissa Nicholson

Cherry Nut Muffins

Ingredients:
1 cup flour
1¼ cup quick-cooking oats, uncooked
¾ cup light brown sugar, packed
1½ tsp. baking powder
½ tsp. salt
1 egg
¾ cup buttermilk
½ cup canola oil
1 cup fresh, pitted cherries, quartered
½ cup macadamia nuts, chopped

Directions:
Preheat oven to 400 degrees.

Prepare a 12-cup muffin tin by lining it with muffin liners.

In a large bowl, combine the flour, oats, brown sugar, baking powder, and salt. In a small bowl, lightly beat the egg. Add the buttermilk and oil. Mix well to combine.

Pour the buttermilk mixture into the dry ingredients and mix until just moistened. Fold in cherries and nuts.

Distribute the batter evenly among the 12 prepared muffin cups.

Bake for 20–22 minutes until slightly golden brown. Transfer individual muffins to a wire rack to cool.

Mexi-beef Lasagna

Day prior to making lasagna:
Make shredded beef—
Trim all fat off boneless rib roast (size depends on amount of meat desired). Season with salt, pepper, and garlic powder. Place in slow cooker. Cover meat with store-bought salsa, either hot or mild, depending on preference. Cook on high until meat begins to pull apart. Continue to shred meat as it cooks. When it's completely done (cooking time depends on size of meat and heat of slow cooker, but about 8 hours), spoon meat from sauce with slotted spoon. Refrigerate.

The next day:
Preheat oven to 350 degrees. Spray 9 x 13 baking dish with nonstick spray.

Mix in a bowl:
Shredded beef from prior day
16 oz. sour cream
15 oz. ricotta cheese
8 oz. diced green chiles (Ortega)
Salt and pepper to taste

1 box lasagna noodles, prepared as directed on box

Grated cheese mixture:
4 cups grated pepper Jack cheese

4 cups grated cheddar cheese

Layer ⅓ noodles onto bottom of baking dish.
Place ½ beef mixture on top of noodles.
Layer ⅓ cheese on top of beef mixture.
Repeat.
Layer final ⅓ noodles.
Top with final ⅓ grated cheeses.

Bake uncovered at 350 degrees for 30 minutes. Broil for a few minutes to brown.

Strawberry Éclair Cake

Crust:
1 cup water
½ cup butter
1 cup flour
1 tsp. sugar
4 eggs
½ tsp. vanilla

Boil water and butter together in a medium saucepan on stove. Then take it off the heat and add the flour and sugar and mix with hand mixer. Add and beat in eggs one at a time. Add in vanilla.
Spread in a lightly greased 9x13 pan.
Bake at 400 degrees for 25 minutes; the cake will not be smooth or uniform in appearance.
Let cool completely.

Filling:
1 (3.4 oz.) box instant French vanilla pudding
2 cups milk
4 oz. Cool Whip, thawed, about ½ of an 8 oz. container
Whisk instant pudding and milk together. Fold in Cool Whip. Let stand for 2-3 minutes
Spread over cooled crust.

Layer on 1 pound sliced strawberries mixed with ½ cup sugar.

Top with 4 oz. Cool Whip, thawed. Drizzle with chocolate syrup. Refrigerate.

Lemon Cheesecake

Crust:
2 cups graham cracker crumbs
1 cup chopped pecans
2 tbs. sugar
½ cup butter or margarine, melted

Filling:
3 pkgs. (8 oz. each) cream cheese, softened
1½ cups granulated sugar
⅓ cup whipping cream
1 tbs. lemon
3 eggs

Topping:
1 cup sugar
2 tbs. flour
3 tbs. cornstarch
Pinch of salt
1½ cups water
⅓ cup lemon juice (from about 2 lemons)
2 tbs. butter
4 egg yolks, beaten

Instructions:
Heat oven to 350 degrees. In small bowl, mix crust ingredients. Press firmly in bottom of greased 9 x 13 baking pan. Bake 10 minutes. Cool completely. Lower heat to 325 degrees.

Filling:
Cream together all ingredients and pour over crust. Bake 60 minutes or until set.

Lemon topping:
In a medium saucepan, whisk together sugar, flour, cornstarch, and salt. Stir in water, lemon juice. Cook over medium-high heat, stirring frequently, until mixture comes to a boil. Stir in butter. Place egg yolks in a small bowl and gradually whisk in ½ cup of hot sugar mixture. Whisk egg yolk mixture back into remaining sugar mixture. Bring to a boil and continue to cook while stirring constantly until thick. Remove from heat. Pour filling onto baked cheesecake.

Date and Nut Bars

Submitted by Bobby Tobey

Ingredients:

4 eggs, well beaten
2 cups chopped pitted dates (measure after chopping)
¼ cup flour
1 tsp. baking powder
2 cups chopped walnuts (measure after chopping)
2 cups sugar
½ tsp. salt

Mix all ingredients in the order listed, stirring well each time. Use electric mixer for eggs only; all other ingredients should be mixed by hand.

Put into a greased and floured 9 x 13 baking pan. Bake at 350 degrees for about 25 minutes or until deep golden brown.

Cool and cut into squares with a plastic knife. Roll in powdered sugar.

Makes about 24 squares.

Picnic Summer Slaw

Submitted by Joanne Kocourek

A tangy vinaigrette dressing is simmered and poured over cabbage, cucumbers, and tomatoes for a refreshing slaw that is perfect for picnics. Easy to prepare and not typical of those commonly made.

Ingredients:

1 (10 oz.) pkg. shredded cabbage
1 cucumber, peeled and chopped
1 green bell pepper, chopped (optional)
1 large tomato, peeled and chopped
1 bunch green onions, chopped
½ cup white sugar
½ cup vegetable oil
¼ cup white vinegar
Salt and ground black pepper to taste

Combine cabbage, cucumber, green bell pepper, tomato, and green onions in a large bowl.

Cook and stir sugar, vegetable oil, vinegar, salt, and pepper together in a saucepan over medium heat until sugar dissolves, about 5 minutes. Remove from heat and allow to cool. Pour marinade over vegetables and stir to coat. Marinate slaw in the refrigerator for at least 2 hours.

The Ultimate Baked Beans

Submitted by Janel Flynn

Great anytime. Perfect for potluck or picnics. Better than your average baked beans. My mother gave me this recipe and I love it!

6 slices bacon, cut up
1 cup chopped onion (1 large), I prefer red onion
1 clove garlic, minced
1 16 oz. can lima beans, rinsed and drained
1 16 oz. can pork and beans in tomato sauce
1 15½ oz. can red kidney beans, rinsed and drained
1 15 oz. can chickpeas, rinsed and drained
1 15 oz. can butter beans, drained
¾ cup ketchup
½ cup molasses
¼ cup brown sugar, packed
1 tbs. prepared mustard
1 tbs. Worcestershire sauce

In a skillet, cook up bacon, onion, and garlic until bacon is crisp and onion is tender. Drain.

In a large bowl, combine onion mix, all the beans, ketchup, molasses, brown sugar, mustard, and Worcestershire sauce.

Transfer to at least a 3-qt. Crock-Pot. Let simmer for 10 to 12 hours on low heat or 4 to 5 hours on high heat.

Serve and enjoy!

Baked Chicken

Submitted by Sandra Kerr

My boyfriend's mom gave me this recipe. I make it every week because it's easy and scrumptious.

Ingredients:

½ cup butter
1 cup corn flakes
1 cup Parmesan cheese
1 pkt. Hidden Valley Ranch dressing
6 boneless and skinless chicken breasts

Melt butter and set aside.

Crush corn flakes, add Parmesan cheese and ranch dressing, and stir well.

Dip each breast in butter, then coat with corn flake mixture.

Place in a glass pan and bake at 375 degrees for 45 minutes, then broil for 5 minutes or until golden brown on top.

Grilled Apricot Pie

Submitted by Vivian Shane

I like this recipe because after you grill a steak for dinner, dessert can be cooking on the BBQ while you eat!

Ingredients:

½ of a 15 oz. pkg. of rolled refrigerated unbaked pie crust (1 crust)
¼ cup brown sugar, packed
2 tsp. flour
⅛ tsp. ground cardamom
⅛ tsp. chili powder
1 lb. (5–6) apricots, halved and pitted, or two 15 oz. cans apricot halves in light syrup, drained
¾ cup granola with raisins
2 tbs. pecan halves
1 disposable foil pan approx. 7⅛ x 5 ⅜ x 1⅛ (this is a common size found in most stores; if you can't get the exact size, just purchase a pan as close to this size as you can get)
Vanilla bean ice cream, optional

Bring pie crust to room temperature per package directions. In a medium bowl, combine brown sugar, flour, cardamom, and chili powder. Add the apricots, gently tossing until coated, and set aside (if the mixture with fresh apricots seems dry, let stand for 10 minutes before use). In another bowl, combine granola and nuts and set aside. Spray disposable foil pan with nonstick cooking spray. Ease the crust into the pan, gently pressing into the sides and corners and allowing the edges to hang over the side of the foil pan (do not trim; leaving the crust with its irregularly shaped edges, which adds to the charm of the pie when it's folded in over the filing). Spoon the apricot mixture into the pan. Sprinkle with the granola mix and fold crust edges over filling.

Preheat gas grill (unless you already used it for dinner). Set heat to medium and adjust for indirect cooking per manufacturer's directions. Place the foil pan on grill rack away from heat. Close cover and grill for 40 minutes or until pie crust is golden brown, fresh fruit is tender, and filling is bubbly. Remove foil pan from the grill and cool for 45 minutes before serving warm, with vanilla bean ice cream if desired.

Kindergarten Cookies

Submitted by Melissa Nicholson

This recipe came from my kindergarten class (I won't say how many years ago). We made them in class (our classroom actually had burners). I remember standing on a stool and stirring. It has been a family favorite since then.

Ingredients:

1 cube butter
2 cups sugar
½ cup milk
Pinch of salt
3 tbs. cocoa
1 tsp. vanilla
3 cups quick oats

Combine butter, sugar, milk, salt, and cocoa. Bring to rolling boil. Continue cooking, while stirring vigorously, for 1 minute. Remove from heat and add vanilla and oats and stir until it begins to cool. Drop by teaspoonful onto waxed paper. Let set. (I usually can't wait and start trying to peel them off to eat too soon.)

Books by Kathi Daley

Come for the murder, stay for the romance.

Buy them on Amazon today.

Zoe Donovan Cozy Mystery:

Halloween Hijinks

The Trouble With Turkeys

Christmas Crazy

Cupid's Curse

Big Bunny Bump-off

Beach Blanket Barbie

Maui Madness

Derby Divas

Haunted Hamlet

Turkeys, Tuxes, and Tabbies

Christmas Cozy

Alaskan Alliance

Matrimony Meltdown

Soul Surrender—*May 2015*

Heavenly Honeymoon—*June 2015*

Ghostly Graveyard – *October 2015*

Santa Sleuth – *December 2015*

Ashton Falls Cozy Cookbook

Paradise Lake Cozy Mystery:

Pumpkins in Paradise
Snowmen in Paradise
Bikinis in Paradise
Christmas in Paradise
Puppies in Paradise
Halloween in Paradise – *August 2015*

Whales and Tails Cozy Mystery:

Romeow and Juliet
The Mad Catter
Grimm's Furry Tail
Legend of Tabby Hollow – *September 2015*
Cat of Christmas Past – *November 2015*

Seacliff High Mystery:

The Secret
The Curse—*May 2015*
The Relic—*July 2015*
The Conspiracy – *October 2015*

Road to Christmas Romance:

Road to Christmas Past

Kathi Daley lives with her husband, kids, grandkids, and Bernese mountain dogs in beautiful Lake Tahoe. When she isn't writing, she likes to read (preferably at the beach or by the fire), cook (preferably something with chocolate or cheese), and garden (planting and planning, not weeding). She also enjoys spending time on the water when she's not hiking, biking, or snowshoeing the miles of desolate trails surrounding her home.

Kathi uses the mountain setting in which she lives, along with the animals (wild and domestic) that share her home, as inspiration for her cozy mysteries.

Stay up-to-date with her newsletter, *The Daley Weekly*. There's a link to sign up on both her Facebook page and her website, or you can access the sign-in sheet at: http://eepurl.com/NRPDf

Visit Kathi:
Facebook at Kathi Daley Books,
www.facebook.com/kathidaleybooks

Kathi Daley Teen –
www.facebook.com/kathidaleyteen

Kathi Daley Books Group Page –
https://www.facebook.com/groups/5695788231468
50/

Kathi Daley Books Birthday Club—get a book on your birthday–
https://www.facebook.com/groups/1040638412628912/

Kathi Daley Recipe Exchange -
https://www.facebook.com/groups/752806778126428/

Webpage - www.kathidaley.com

E-mail - kathidaley@kathidaley.com

Recipe Submission E-mail –
kathidaleyrecipes@kathidaley.com

Goodreads:
https://www.goodreads.com/author/show/7278377.Kathi_Daley

Twitter at Kathi Daley@kathidaley -
https://twitter.com/kathidaley

Tumblr - http://kathidaleybooks.tumblr.com/

Amazon Author Page -
http://www.amazon.com/Kathi-Daley/e/B00F3BOX4K/ref=sr_tc_2_0?qid=1418237358&sr=8-2-ent

Pinterest - http://www.pinterest.com/kathidaley/

20239999R00107

Made in the USA
San Bernardino, CA
03 April 2015